THE EVANGELINE SERIES

HENRY

ASTRID AURELIUS

First published by Astrid Aurelius - Independent Author 2022

This novel is entirely a work of fiction. The names, characters and incidents portrayed in it are the work of the author's imagination. Any resemblance to actual persons, living or dead, events or localities is entirely coincidental.

Designations used by companies to distinguish their products are often claimed as trademarks. All brand names and product names used in this book and on its cover are trade names, service marks, trademarks and registered trademarks of their respective owners. The publishers and the book are not associated with any product or vendor mentioned in this book. None of the companies referenced within the book have endorsed the book.

First edition

ISBN (eBook): 978-1-7366951-9-7

ISBN (Paperback): 979-8-9855363-0-0

ISBN (Hardback): 979-8-9855363-1-7

Cover art by Lena Yang

Editing by Tiffany Andrea

CHAPTER 1

LONDON

"Hullo?"

"Is Pravin Nagra available?"

"Speaking."

"Hi, Mr. Nagra. This is Elise with The Baxter Group. Is this a good time?"

Pravin was lounging in front of the television but sat up straight at the mention of The Baxter Group. "Yes, of course," he replied cordially. "How can I help?"

The woman notified him he had been hired and was slotted for the next training group starting in two weeks. "But we can put you in a subsequent training group if the notice is too short. We do recognize that you are not currently living in the United States."

"No, no. I can make the move. It's no trouble at all."

"Great. The details of your offer are on the way. We look forward to receiving your confirmation."

Pravin smiled. "I'll send it straight away."

"Welcome to The Baxter Group, Mr. Nagra. Have a great day."

"Thank you. Thank you very much. Cheers."

After he hung up, Pravin stood and glanced around his flat, quickly feeling overwhelmed by the timeline he just agreed to. He was about to tap 'Mum' on his contact list to share the news when he heard a knock on his door.

He stepped over to the door and opened it, shocked by the face that greeted him.

"Hello, son. It's been a while."

Pravin's widened eyes finally budged from his father's face when he poked his head into the hallway, looking left and right. "Dad? What are you doing here? Did anyone see you?" he asked, panicked, as he opened the door wide to grant him entry.

"Relax, Geoffrey. No one saw me. And even if they had, no one knows who I am." The man with mostly black hair—peppered with white—and dark green eyes entered, nonchalant as usual. He had a full beard, and the coloring was the same as the hair on his head.

"I wish you wouldn't drop in like this, Dad. And I wish you wouldn't call me that, either." Pravin closed the door firmly after again looking out into the corridor to confirm it was empty.

"My apologies. I'm in London for business and wanted to see how you were doing."

Pravin didn't see his dad often, but when he did, it always made him a nervous wreck. If anyone found out he was the son of The Crocodile—a notorious criminal and pseudo-terrorist—his career would be over. He wanted nothing to do with Henry's nefarious activities, and he felt uneasy with his dad showing up at his flat unannounced.

Pravin sighed and stepped into his small kitchen. "Care for a drink?" He observed his father examining the art hanging on the wall in the lounge.

"Actually, yes. Thank you." He glanced at Pravin over his shoulder before returning his eyes to the art.

Pravin knew his dad liked scotch, so he poured a moderate amount into two glasses, leaving the kitchen to approach him in the lounge.

"How's your mother?" he asked as he accepted a glass from Pravin.

Pravin brought his tumbler to his lips. "She's well." He took a sip. It irked him when his father asked about his mother. He was too small when his parents split to understand why his dad left, but he'd observed his mother enough to know that his leaving had hurt her.

Henry's eyes dropped as he drank his scotch. "So what's new in your life?"

Pravin slid his phone into his pocket. "Actually...I just received word that I've been hired on at an American contracting firm. I have two weeks to get to DC and get settled."

"Oh?" His father's eyebrows arched. "Why are you leaving MI6? You're still clean, right? You haven't slipped with the drugs, have you?"

"Yes, Dad; I haven't relapsed." After taking another sip of scotch, Pravin's eyes fell to his glass.

"I'd just like a change of scenery, primarily." He thought about *her* for a moment and a feeling similar to a vice around his rib cage distracted him for a moment, but he made sure his face was neutral. "I spoke to my superiors some time back about the change I wanted to make. They understood and were supportive."

"What's the name of the firm you're going to?" his dad inquired casually.

"The Baxter Group."

His father raised the glass to his mouth and hesitated before taking a long sip. "The *Baxter* Group?" he asked, as if confirming.

Pravin nodded. "Several of my colleagues at MI6 have worked with them in joint operations and have always had positive things to say."

"Indeed." Henry's face was blank. "I'm familiar with The Baxter Group."

Pravin's eyes darted to the side as he wondered how much longer his dad would stay, noticing that his scotch was almost empty already. He opened his mouth, prepared to ask if he'd like more, when his father spoke again.

"I can help you get settled in DC. I own a building there...in a very desirable part of the city, no less. Just say the word and I can arrange for it to be set up for you."

"Really?" A warm feeling of hope swelled inside him, but then he reined it back in and coughed awkwardly. "I'm not sure, Dad. You know I don't want to be traced to you...I can't be traced to you. That would be worse than my former drug habit coming to light. It would ruin me."

"I've owned the building for years and no one has ever been the wiser. It's a condo building...a rehabbed warehouse from the turn of the twentieth century. Let's just say it's one of my *legitimate* sources of income." His dad's lips tilted as he brought the tumbler to his mouth to finish what remained of his scotch.

Pravin scratched his scalp. "Let me think about it."

A moment later, Pravin observed as his father stepped over to a chair and casually sat.

"There's something I need to talk to you about, Geof—Pravin."

The change in Henry's demeanor was substantial. Before he sat, he was cool and casual. But now, as he sat, he seemed troubled, and Pravin felt his face twist in concern. "What is it?"

"I want to tell you everything...to explain why...I do what I do." His dad spoke slowly, pausing awkwardly, which wasn't like him. "There are few people who know the entire story. Not even your mother knows."

Pravin sunk in a chair opposite his dad, finding himself intrigued by what he was about to learn. "Okay, Dad. Let's hear it."

CHAPTER 2

ORIGINS

On February 7, 1962, Henry Thomas Coats was born at home in his parents' Manhattan brownstone. His father, Geoffrey, stayed by his wife's side for the birth, something that was virtually unheard of at the time. He held his son, freshly cleaned and swaddled, moments after he was born, handing him to his beloved wife, Elizabeth. They were both in their late thirties when Henry was born. They believed Elizabeth was barren, since she had never conceived in all their years together. Geoffrey traveled often for work, but he took a month off, needing a break, and wanting to spend some quality time with his wife. Lo-and-behold, she got pregnant. Turns out they just weren't timing things right.

Geoffrey was an attorney who specialized in international business law, so he would be hired by companies all over Europe and the Caribbean to serve as a consultant. After Henry was born, he wanted to maintain a presence in his life, so he convinced Elizabeth to sell the brownstone and they relocated as a family to various foreign countries.

The first after Henry was born was France, and they lived there for just under two years. Henry's first words were in French. After France, they moved to Switzerland, where Henry was exposed to both French and German. They lived in Switzerland for nine months before moving to Munich, Germany.

Henry would often encounter his mother sitting by herself, crying; he would ask "Mama, why are you sad?" She would never answer him; she would just open her arms, he would enter them, and she would hold him and tell him how much she loved him. He knew it was true. As a boy, he never had to wonder if his parents loved him; he knew they did.

The family had lived in Munich for two years, when Geoffrey was offered a very high-paying job in Moscow. While living in Moscow, Henry started schooling. He attended a prestigious boys' academy with the sons of Russian aristocrats, government officials, and other wealthy Russians. His peers liked him very much, and his teachers thought him very smart. He picked up the Russian language easily, already fluent in English, French, and German.

He was nine years old when his mother gave birth to a baby girl, but because of complications, neither of them survived. His father was devastated, and Henry didn't fully understand yet that he would never see his beloved mother again or meet his baby sister, Charlotte.

The death of his wife and baby girl drove Geoffrey to leave his job in Moscow and return to New York City, where he buried Elizabeth and Charlotte. Geoffrey and Henry remained in New York from then on. Geoffrey obtained a lucrative position at an investment banking firm housed in the north tower of the World Trade Center shortly after it opened.

Henry attended a private school and when he was fifteen years old, he got a job at the Metropolitan Museum of Art as a ticket collector. He didn't need a job at all, but he wanted to work at the museum to learn more about art. After being introduced to the museum during a school field trip, he felt nostalgic for the art he encountered often when he lived in Europe. He eventually worked his way up to the gift shop, and he was allowed to walk around the museum after closing time to look at the various exhibits.

He was primarily drawn to the Classic European paintings and sculptures. It was during his time at The Met that he embraced his passion for art and historical artifacts. He decided to pursue a career in art and anthropology and applied to, and was accepted by, many Ivy league schools, including Harvard, Columbia, Yale, and Oxford. He missed Europe, so he decided on Oxford, which would allow him easy access to travel the rest of Europe while in school.

Henry was a very handsome young man with deep green eyes, black hair, and a light olive complexion. He had no problems finding female companionship, but none of the women he encountered tempted him into monogamy.

Through his studies, he learned about art restoration, art appraisal, art inspections, verifying originals versus imitations or reproductions, and everything in between. His anthropology studies allowed him to learn about Eurasian culture and the evolution of cultures over the years, as evinced in the artifacts studied. He graduated with his master's degree when he was twenty-four years old and was immediately hired by the National Gallery in London. His position charged him with traveling all over Europe, and sometimes the US, to scout private art collections for pieces to loan to the National Gallery. When he did go to the US, he often ended up in New York and would take advantage of the time to visit with his father and take flowers to the grave where his mother and sister rested.

Chapter 3

Career Choices

Henry had been working for the National Gallery for three years when he was sent to the Cayman Islands to inspect the art collection owned by a British expat living there. He learned that this man, Philip Casper, was widely traveled, having served as an unofficial diplomat for the Crown years before. Just like everyone else, the man instantly liked Henry and called him "Hank". Henry took an inventory of the art collection and provided Philip with an appraisal. The art collection was large, and it took Henry almost a whole week to perform a thorough inspection. As he was preparing to leave, Philip offered Henry a job as his estate manager. He offered to pay him a salary triple what the National Gallery paid him, as well as house him in a private ocean-facing villa on the property.

The salary increase was tempting. He believed the National Gallery wasn't paying him what he deserved, but he loved his job so much that he made it work, mainly by being supplemented by his Father's money. He asked Philip if he could think about it and let him know.

On his last night in Grand Cayman, after dinner, he took a walk on the beach near his hotel. It was warm, and the air was fresh. He thought about London and the culture of Europe and how much he loved it there, but then he thought about the winters and the dreary days, contrasting it to the year-round sunshine on the island. He wondered what kind of vacation time he would have in this role, because he would still want to travel and experience the world.

While he was walking, he came upon a young Indian woman sitting on the sand with her bare feet in the water. He was instantly taken by her beauty: her long, dark hair; her smooth, brown skin; and her bright smile.

He said 'hello' and she responded in kind. It was then that he realized she was English, hearing her crisp accent. He wanted to talk to her, but felt awkward, and he must have looked it, because she took pity on him and invited him to sit with her. He accepted the invitation and started the conversation by introducing himself, then asking her name and where she was from. She told him her name was Lydia, and she lived in London.

They fell into an easy discussion about life in London; the good, the bad, and the ugly. He learned she worked for the Ministry of Education, and she aspired to work her way up the chain into a prestigious ministry leadership role someday. They learned they both attended Oxford around the same time and couldn't believe their paths had never crossed.

She asked him about his upbringing and where he was from originally, and he explained his experience growing up in different countries. She was impressed by his language skills and wanted to hear him talk about his job at the National Gallery. During the conversation, she disclosed that she had been adopted as an infant from an orphanage in India.

They talked about literature and poetry, and she recited a love poem in French, explaining how beautiful and heartbreaking the words were.

Henry was smitten with her and boldly kissed her. She returned the kiss and asked him if his hotel was nearby. He told her it was, and she asked him to take her there.

He made love to her tenderly at first, and then passionately, as they both felt an undeniable mutual attraction to each other. When he woke up the next morning, she was gone, but had left him a note thanking him for the beautiful night, hoping that they would meet again someday.

Though he wished he could have told her goodbye and gotten her phone number, he knew her name and where she worked, so he resolved to find her when he returned to London. Because of this, he returned to Philip's estate to thank him for the job offer, but respectfully decline it.

He knocked at the door of the main house of the grand estate but froze in shock when Lydia answered.

CHAPTER 4

FATE STEPS IN

They stared at each other for a long moment, neither of them able to find words to say when Philip approached. "Lydia, darling, who is it?" Philip appeared at the door and saw Henry. "Ah! Hank! I'm so glad to see you this morning. Allow me to introduce you to my daughter, Lydia. She's just arrived from London late last night."

Henry's face finally responded to his brain commanding him to smile and rejoice after the initial shock wore off. He held out a hand, looking into her eyes. "Very pleased to meet you, Lydia." She smiled back, took his hand, and he kissed her knuckles gently, noting that she smelled like roses.

"Lydia, this is the chap I told you about this morning. I offered him a job." Philip motioned for Henry to come inside.

"Papa, you didn't..." she started, but cut herself off. "Of course, Papa." She glanced sideways at Henry with a dark flush on her cheeks.

"Well, my boy; have you had enough time to think about my offer?" Philip asked as they stepped into the parlor near the front door.

Henry was thoroughly confused and conflicted. "I have thought about it, Sir, but...I have questions." He couldn't help but glance at Lydia as he replied.

Her eyes were wide, and she looked somewhat panicked.

"Then let's talk. Follow me." Philip turned on his heel and walked down the hallway, leading Henry to a plush study.

Henry looked over his shoulder at Lydia, who followed as well, and he wondered why she looked so spooked. Was she not happy to see him?

Philip stood at the window, looking out at the ocean beyond. He picked up a crystal carafe and poured the golden liquid into a short stemmed, balloon-vesseled glass. "Can I offer you some cognac?" Philip looked at Henry.

Henry put his hands in his pockets. "Yes, please. Thank you, Sir."

"Lydia?" Philip's eyes moved from Henry to Lydia.

"No thank you, Papa."

As Philip poured the cognac, Henry turned to Lydia. "So, Lydia, do you travel here often?"

"Well—" she started, but Philip interrupted.

"Not often enough; I've been trying for years to convince her to move here." Philip handed a glass to Henry. "But she prefers her life in London."

Lydia peered at Henry. "Papa doesn't understand my career aspirations."

"I thought I'd have you married off by now, but since you aren't, why not come take care of your

Papa?" Philip's eyes were smiling as he brought his glass to his lips.

Lydia's cheeks blushed anew, and she sighed, looking defeated.

Henry registered her discomfort and tried to think of something to say to help. "Well, Lydia, I commend you for following your passion. There are many who don't and lead miserable lives because of it."

Philip's face fell and his eyes went glassy. Henry noticed the change and feared he had offended him. Philip looked at his glass, then at Lydia and Henry.

"Lydia, darling? When did you get here?" Philip looked confused as his eyes traveled the room. "How did I get in here?"

"Oh, Papa..." Lydia rushed to her father's side, taking the cognac glass out of his hands, giving it to Henry. "Please sit down, Papa." She urged him to a tufted leather armchair nearby.

"Lydia, it's so good to see you! Where's your mama? Lucy?" he called out.

"Papa...it's alright." She knelt down beside his chair and held his hand.

"Lydia, I'm tired. Please send for Bosley...please send for my steward."

"Papa...Bosley isn't here anymore. I'll help you to bed, okay?"

"What do you mean, he's not here anymore? Where in bloody hell did he go?" he asked, agitated. "Bosley!"

Henry watched wide-eyed, deducing that Philip was having some sort of dementia episode. He had heard of them but had never witnessed one before.

"Papa, please let me help you," Lydia spoke softly and stroked the back of his hand. "Please, Papa."

Lydia's attempts to soothe her father were successful. Philip rose out of the chair and Lydia led him to the door with a hand on his elbow. Philip's eyes fell on Henry as if for the first time. "Who are you?"

Henry glanced at Lydia, then made eye contact with Philip. "My name is Henry, Sir. Pleasure to meet you," he responded with a smile.

"Ah, Henry! A good name. But can I call you Hank?"

"Papa, let's get you to bed," Lydia said, urging him onward, glancing at Henry. "Please wait here," she whispered as they left the room.

Henry stood in the middle of the study holding two cognac glasses, feeling worried about Philip and sympathy for Lydia. Almost twenty minutes later, she returned, closing the office door behind her. She looked distressed and, without a word, took one of the cognac glasses from Henry and drank its contents in one tilt.

Henry's unblinking eyes locked on her as he brought his glass to his lips and sipped. "Is he okay?"

Lydia sighed. "He will be. I'm sorry you saw that. I knew this morning he would have an episode. I had to remind him multiple times at breakfast that I had already finished with university and I was working in London."

"I see." Henry nodded, keeping his eyes on her. "Is that why you seemed so startled earlier?"

"Yes. This was a very tame episode. He's had some violent ones in the past."

"Ah...I was afraid that maybe..." he paused, regarding the liquid in his glass thoughtfully. "Maybe you weren't happy to see me."

A slow grin brightened Lydia's face. "Did you not find my note?"

"No, I found it."

"Well, then you know I hoped we'd meet again. I just never dreamt it would be so soon. Or here."

Henry felt sheepish. "How long has he had... this?"

Lydia sighed. "He started showing symptoms about two years ago. Bosley, his old steward, contacted me at work one day to let me know that something was very wrong with Papa. Bosley had never heard of dementia before, much less seen it in action."

"It's a cruel disease," Henry observed.

She nodded. "It is, indeed. I've given up on trying to remind him that Mama died five years ago."

"I'm sorry for your loss," Henry said solemnly.

She smiled at him, but it was a sad smile. "I appreciate the kind words, but I've done my grieving. I miss her, but she lived a hard life, and..." she stopped and hesitated. "So...my father offered you a job? Doing what, may I ask?"

"He said it would be managing the estate," Henry replied neutrally.

"Did he...explain his business?" She seemed uncomfortable asking the question.

"No. I wasn't aware he had a business. I'm here to evaluate his art collection. He sent a request to the National Gallery weeks ago asking for an appraisal because he was considering loaning parts of his collection to the museum. So they sent me here," Henry explained. "I assumed he was retired. My supervisor at the Gallery told me he was an unofficial diplomat for England years ago."

"An *unofficial* diplomat? That's a new one," she said ruefully. "Well, he was an *actual* diplomat about twenty years ago. But somewhere along the way, he developed an appetite for the privileges his diplomat status afforded him, and he saw an opportunity to make money." She shook her head. "He kept it very quiet, but at some point, the scheme was revealed. He was stripped of his diplomat status, and even though he should have been punished for taking advantage of his authority, he was never charged with anything. My assumption is that he knew about some secret skeletons that allowed him to escape unscathed. That seems to be how it works when you are so intertwined with government officials."

Henry set down his cognac glass. "So even though he lost his privileges, that didn't stop him from continuing his...his..." Henry hesitated before continuing. "What exactly was he doing?"

Lydia's eyes traveled around the well-appointed room. "It started out relatively harmless: Cuban cigars; Russian vodka; Persian rugs; Chinese jade. He found a way to avoid the taxes and tariffs that usually come with importing those items...not to mention any embargo issues. He made loads of money selling the stock he transported. But then it escalated after he lost his privileges. My mother told me once that it wasn't his fault; that some people he was doing business with threatened him...threatened us; they forced him to move things for them. Drugs, weapons, people. It made her sick with worry and shame. My father is a good man who made some terrible choices. He took it further when, out of desperation to keep us safe, he hired a team of mercenaries to strike first against the ones threatening us." Lydia sighed. "As an extra measure to protect me, he had my name changed to my Indian birth name. So, in the English census, I am Priya Nagra; but to those I care about, I am Lydia Casper."

Henry took a step closer to her. "And to this day, he continues transporting these things? Was he not successful in removing the threat to his family?"

"No, he was; but he was in too deep after that. He crossed a line he couldn't uncross." Her eyes filled with tears.

Henry scratched his cheek. This was a lot to process. Philip asked him to manage his estate, but based on what Lydia was saying, that would mean being involved in an illegal enterprise. "Last night, you told me your name was Lydia. How were you so certain you could trust me?"

She smiled and her brown eyes sparkled. "You were so awkward." She chuckled. "You didn't exactly fit the bill of an assassin. I assumed you were a tourist. I didn't see the harm in sharing my preferred name."

Henry smiled back at her. "I want to help, but I don't know what to do."

Lydia shook her head. "Neither do I. I just wish all of this would go away. I wish my father could return to England and live a normal life, but that can never happen."

The wheels were turning in Henry's mind as he tried to reason through this. Maybe he could help...maybe as the estate manager, he could slow down the business and eventually dismantle it, ensuring Philip had enough money to maintain his lifestyle, as well as get the care that he needs. He took another step closer to her. "Look, I have to get back to London. Can you please let your father know I am considering his offer?"

Lydia's face held traces of concern. "Are you sure you want to get involved in this? You seem like a good man, and I would hate for your life to be marred by my father's misdeeds."

"Maybe it doesn't have to be that way...maybe I can help your father retire."

"I wish it were that simple. And I don't mean for this to sound morbid, but he'll eventually have to retire anyway when his disease takes him." Lydia shook her head. "Please, just forget about all of this and move on with your life, Henry."

Henry's eyes searched hers and he reached out to touch her face, but stopped himself short. "I don't want to forget."

"Henry..." she whispered. "I'll be back in London in three weeks. Take me to dinner?" She smiled at him.

He beamed back. "I would love to."

"Let's exchange numbers." Lydia handed Henry a small white notecard from her father's desk and a heavy pen. She wrote her number down on a separate card and handed it to him, accepting a card from him in return. She smiled at him again. "I look forward to seeing you in London."

He looked at her lips and grinned. "Likewise." He glanced at his watch. "I need to get going if I'm going to catch my flight." He slowly exited the study and walked to the front door.

Lydia followed closely behind him. He opened the front door, and she touched him on the shoulder. He faced her, and she stepped in close to him, then pressed her lips to his. "Goodbye, Henry," she said after the kiss.

"Goodbye, Lydia," he replied with a smile.

CHAPTER 5

THE SPEED OF LIFE

Henry traveled back to London and spent the next weeks thinking of Lydia often. He was eager to see her again and hoped that she would bring a good report of her father's condition. He had told her he intended to consider the job offer, but the more he thought of it, the more uneasy it made him to enter a world like that, regardless of how much money he would make. While he wished he could help the problem go away, he wouldn't know the first place to start.

The day Lydia was to return to London arrived, and he went to work that morning with great anticipation. He wanted to call her first thing, but recognized it was possible that her plane wouldn't land until later in the day, so he resolved to wait until she reached out. It was near the end of the day, and he was in the middle of overseeing the restoration efforts of a long-displayed portrait, when his supervisor approached him. "Henry, there's someone here asking to see you."

"Asking to see me?" Henry had never gotten a visitor at work before, so it caught him off guard.

"Yes; she's waiting in the Central Hall."

"She?" Henry clarified. "Thank you." He looked at his watch and addressed the person working on the painting. "Let's stop here today." Then he turned to his supervisor. "Do you mind if I have an early exit?"

His supervisor looked at his watch. "Oh, it's close enough. Go on, Henry," he answered with a gap-toothed smile.

Henry made haste through the exhibits to the Central Hall. He saw her immediately, though her back was turned to him. He approached and softly touched her shoulder. "Lydia?" he said, unable to halt the smile from seizing his face.

She turned and faced him with a smile, though her eyes were red-rimmed; she'd been crying. "Hello, Henry."

Henry was immediately concerned. "It's good to see you." He paused. "Is everything okay?"

Though she attempted to brighten the smile on her face, her composure crumbled like an ancient stone wall and a sob burst from her lips. She shook her head. "Papa..." she started and took a deep breath. "Papa is dead."

The revelation left Henry in shock. This was not the news he was hoping for. He reached out and pulled her into his arms, attempting to soothe her the best he could as her cheek pressed against his shoulder. "I'm so sorry, Lydia. Do you mind if I ask what happened?"

She asked if they could go somewhere to talk, and Henry told her there was a pub nearby that was usually tame and quiet. They walked to the pub and took a seat at a table in the back corner. She ordered a cup of Earl Grey; he ordered a pint, and she started crying again. She took a few deep breaths, clearly trying to calm herself enough to speak. "After you left, I learned from the staff that his episodes were becoming more and more frequent. As soon as he was lucid again, I brought it up with him and begged him to seek treatment. He was in denial at first but was faced with evidence of his downward spiral when I showed him a portrait of Mama that he ruined during one of his more violent fits. He had apparently convinced himself—when he couldn't find her once—that she had left him for another man." Lydia closed her eyes and a tear rolled down each cheek.

"So again, I begged him to seek treatment. I had heard of a doctor in New York who could evaluate him and possibly slow the progression of his disease. I told him I would go with him to New York and be by his side for the consultation. I told him to sell everything and leave the Island and take up residence in New York, promising him I could visit more often...it is much easier to get to New York from London, than to the Cayman Islands." She paused and took a deep breath. "He started sobbing and apologized for being such a burden. I pleaded with him to not feel that way and I urged him to walk away from this life that had taken control of him and start fresh in New

York." She swallowed and looked into Henry's face. "Then he asked about you. He asked if you had considered his job offer. And I got angry with him...telling him it wasn't right to send a good man down that path unwittingly. I admonished him for making the offer to you and not disclosing the full nature of what you would have to manage. I told him I hoped you would turn him down, because I couldn't bear the idea of another life being ruined by his business." She closed her eyes and bit her lip. When she reopened her eyes, they were full of fresh tears that were spilling over.

"Then he told me I was right...that he didn't blame me for hating him for what he put me and Mama through." She sobbed and continued, "Then he told me he would think about New York and would give me an answer before I returned to London."

Henry listened intently, resting a hand on her shoulder as his thumb stroked her skin consolingly.

She swallowed and continued. "That night...he must have had another episode, or something, because he took a fistful of sleeping pills." Her body shook as she cried, and she leaned her head onto Henry's shoulder as she wept.

"I'm so sorry, Lydia," was all Henry could think to say.

Several moments later, she pulled her head back and smiled at him sadly. "As we were preparing for the funeral, a group of men I had never met before stormed into the house, demanding to see Papa. Since I didn't know who they were, I swiftly became Priya Nagra, a servant in the house; I even tried out the Indian accent I've been working on so they would overlook me. It was fine until their leader said he would start shooting people until the new person in charge stepped up." She sighed. "I didn't know what to do...I certainly didn't want anyone to be shot, but I didn't want to reveal myself either. So I told them Philip had not named a successor." She paused. "They didn't like that and killed two people." She shook her head. "They left but warned us they would return and would shoot more people unless there was someone who would talk business with them." She sighed and wiped the tears from her face with her fingers. "They returned the day of the funeral and started threatening us again. I didn't know what else to do, so I told them I would try to help them. But they were obstinate...saying they wouldn't get what they wanted from a servant. I told them I could help them and to please tell me what they needed."

Henry shook his head. "Lydia...you didn't—" He stopped himself short, then continued, "You shouldn't have to get your hands dirty because of your father. Your future is too promising."

Lydia took a ragged breath. "I didn't know what else to do. I felt responsible for those people and I'm certain they were expecting me to do what my father would have done."

"What happened then?" Henry asked, touching her hand.

She paused and her eyes fell to his hand, and her cheeks turned pink. "They demanded that we follow-through with Papa's promise to arrange the transport of a poppy harvest from Afghanistan to their drug producing partner in Burma. I asked him to give me a few days to make the arrangements."

Henry waited patiently for her to continue, hoping that the outcome was positive, but preparing himself for the worst. He could see how distraught she was, and he wished that there was any other solution besides her having to get involved in Philip's business.

"I scoured my father's office looking for anything that could help me arrange the shipment...anything at all. A black book; a ledger; a schedule. As I was flipping through some papers, I came across a picture of my father as a younger man, standing with two other men around the same age. I'm fairly certain they were in Vietnam. I turned it over and read the back, and I couldn't believe my luck. It said *'Call me if your family ever needs protection again'* and it had a phone number. I called the number immediately and told him who I was. He was an American but didn't tell me his name. He was very sad to hear that Papa was dead. I then told him about what was happening, and I asked if there was any way he could help. He assured me he could and told me that a team would be deployed in less than twenty-four hours." She brought her knuckles to her mouth and looked at Henry. "When I hung up with him, I felt like I could breathe for the first time since Papa died. I had no idea what was going to happen, so I sent the staff home. I didn't want to risk them getting caught in the middle of something. I continued looking through Papa's records and found a brown leather book hidden in a false bottom drawer." Lydia sighed. "Papa clearly knew he was losing his grip because this book appeared to be quite a comprehensive account of names, bank accounts, phone numbers, specialties, and locations. I estimated that there were about sixty names in this book, with contact information for people from South Africa to Newfoundland and everywhere in between. The specialties ranged from cocaine to historical artifacts to fossil fuels. He had added your name to the book, Henry, with 'Art' as your specialty."

Henry wasn't sure how he felt about his name being found alongside illegal drug dealers. "I hope the book is safe; I'd hate for someone to get a hold of it and jump to the wrong conclusions."

"Don't worry; I put it in a lockbox at my father's bank," she assured him. "In hindsight, maybe I should have destroyed it, but something told me to save it."

Henry nodded. "What happened next, Lydia?"

"Well, not even twelve hours had passed when I heard the voices of several men outside the house. I thought the drug dealers were back, but when I looked out the window, I could see it wasn't them. And the phone rang. I answered it and the man I spoke to earlier—the American—asked me to confirm that his team had arrived, describing what they should look like. I told him they were outside, and I asked what I should do. He told me to let them in and the leader would provide instructions." She sighed. "Ultimately, the drug dealers returned, and they could never have been prepared for what was waiting for them." She looked at Henry again and her eyes filled with tears. "Those men are dead because of me."

"Lydia," Henry said her name firmly and turned in his chair to face her, putting his hands on her shoulders. "If you hadn't asked for help, you might be dead...along with your father's staff. They were innocent...you are innocent. Those drug dealers were not. I would argue that they chose their fate."

"Henry..." she whispered his name as tears rolled down her cheeks. She leaned toward him, and he met her halfway with a gentle kiss. "Henry?" she whispered his name again.

He looked into her eyes and touched her cheek. "Yes?"

"I'm pregnant." The words left her lips and reached his ears, and they both froze.

Henry felt like he had just stepped off of a poorly assembled carnival ride. His head was spinning, and his stomach felt like it had been turned inside out. "You're pregnant?" he repeated the words mechanically as he looked at her face.

She nodded as another tear rolled down her cheek. "I'm sorry..." she said, covering her face with her hands.

He put his hands on either side of his head in an effort to stop the spinning. "It's...you're...the baby is mine?" he stumbled into the question, struggling with finding the words he wanted to say.

She removed her hands from her face and sniffled. "Yes. You are the father, Henry."

He blinked and his mouth opened, then closed. He didn't know what to say, but she looked terrified. *Was he ready to be a father? Was she ready to be a mother?* he wondered. "Lydia," he said finally, taking her hands. "I'm here for you...however you need or want me to be."

Fresh tears filled her eyes again as she squeezed his hands. "I want this baby, Henry." Her lips and voice trembled.

Henry swallowed hard and his heart grew, prompted by the tenderness he felt for her. He wondered if he loved her; he certainly felt something quite strong for Lydia. She was beautiful and smart, and she needed to be saved from her father's mistakes. Henry wanted to be the one to save her...to be her hero. "So do I," he said at last, touching her cheek with a gentle hand.

Lydia's eyes locked onto Henry's as a smile slowly spread across her lips. "Really?" she replied with gleaming eyes and damp cheeks.

Henry nodded and smiled back at her. "Yes, Lydia. We'll do this together."

Without warning, she flung herself onto him, wrapping her arms around his neck in an embrace; she laughed and cried and covered his face in kisses.

They left the pub shortly thereafter and went to Lydia's flat, where Henry spent the night.

Henry slept fitfully that night, his head replaying the events Lydia described, sometimes exactly, sometimes with an alternate ending where she was shot and killed. He awoke and watched her sleeping peacefully beside him. He needed to make sure she never had to touch Philip's business again, and he thought through his original idea of stepping in and disassembling the business. He resolved to discuss it with her in the morning.

His eyes dropped to her abdomen. From the outside, nothing looked different, but he knew there was a life growing inside her. He reached out and laid a hand gently on her lower belly. She stirred slightly and placed a hand on his. He closed his eyes and went back to sleep.

CHAPTER 6

TEAMWORK

The next morning, over breakfast, Henry told Lydia what he wanted to do. She pushed back, telling him it wasn't necessary. "I released the staff before I left, and I don't care if the place is looted and burned to the ground. I have no plans to ever return."

Henry wanted to agree with her, but he thought about all the amazing art and antiques he saw when he was there. And with Lydia pregnant, the extra income from the sale of some of those items would be helpful to ensure their child could live a comfortable life. "I sympathize with your lack of concern for the place, but...I chose my career because I love art, not because it would make me rich. I want to be able to provide for the baby, but my income is not exactly family-proof yet. Maybe...if you sold a few of your father's art pieces, the money could be set aside for the baby's upbringing."

Lydia sighed and looked contemplative. "That's a very prudent suggestion. Let's be honest, my income isn't the most robust either...and I never accepted financial help from my father. I never wanted to risk anyone in London connecting me to him."

Henry nodded. "Why don't you think about it? I understand wanting to have as few connections as possible to your father's lifestyle, so the decision shouldn't be made lightly."

She chewed on her lip. "Just out of curiosity... how much is my father's art collection worth?"

"My assessment valued it at about twenty-two million pounds," Henry replied. "Just selling two or three pieces will be plenty for a diaper and education fund. The rest you could donate to the National Gallery."

Lydia grinned. "A diaper fund?" She chuckled, then took a deep breath and smiled at him. "You know...you are the first person I've been able to talk to about all of this, apart from my father, anyway. It's such a relief not having to walk on eggshells."

Henry smiled back at her. "Good; I'm glad you trust me." He touched the bare skin on her arm.

Lydia's eyes fell to his hand. "I'll spend today thinking about it and I'll let you know what I decide tonight...assuming you'll come back to me."

"If you want me here, I'll be here," Henry said, then looked at his watch. "I have to go. I need to get ready for work at my place."

"Of course, darling," she said, and her cheeks blushed.

Henry grinned and walked to the door; she followed. At the door, he touched her face. "I'll see you tonight...darling." He winked at her.

"Goodbye, Henry," Lydia replied with a laugh as he left.

Later that night, Henry returned to Lydia's flat and offered to take her out for dinner, as promised on the island. She told him she'd rather have take-away Chinese and offered to call in an order at a nearby place. Henry agreed, so she called it in, and he picked it up. As he was walking back to her flat, he passed a flower stand and bought a small bouquet of bright summer blooms. When he returned to her apartment, he offered her the flowers, as one would do on a proper first date. She laughed and told him they were lovely. As she was putting them in a vase, Henry set out the take-away containers on the dining table where Lydia had set plates and chopsticks.

Over dinner, they talked about their day at work; Henry described a new exhibit they are planning to install in a currently vacant gallery hall, and Lydia talked broadly about a new art program the Ministry was to implement in the secondary schools, which Henry applauded.

They were almost done eating when Lydia told Henry that she thought about what they discussed that morning. "I think you're right. I think it would take some pressure off of us if we can set aside some money for the baby."

Henry set down his chopsticks and focused on her face. "Did your father have a lawyer? I'm assuming he did."

Lydia nodded. "Yes. George Magee. I've been dodging his calls, actually." She sighed. "He's been trying to probate Papa's will."

"Call him and let him know you want to talk to him about what to do with your father's art collection. He can then reach out to the National Gallery, and they'll assign me to oversee the transfer of the art."

"Will you choose the pieces to sell?" she asked. "I don't think I could choose."

"Yes. I'll take care of it. Just let Mr. Magee know I'm helping you, and I can do the rest. I've done this a few times for the National Gallery with other benefactors."

"Maybe in a small way, Papa can have some posthumous redemption for his offenses in life by gifting so much of his beloved art for public appreciation."

"Maybe so..." Henry responded. "But...for your protection...maybe it ought to be an anonymous donation?"

She paused and met his eyes. "You're right. If Philip Casper's name was on a wall in the National Gallery, I'm certain a few eyebrows would be raised." She pushed her plate away. "When you were sent to appraise the collection, they knew who the art belonged to. Do you know how they planned to address it then?"

Henry shook his head. "I don't...but knowing what I know now about his business and the measures taken to protect your identity, I would recommend the anonymous approach. The lawyer can help facilitate that."

"Thank you, Henry." Lydia touched his hand. "Can you stay with me again tonight?" she asked, and her cheeks blushed as her eyes held an unspoken hope.

"Of course I'll stay." But there was something in her gaze…a message he didn't understand. "And I won't even have to rush off in the morning."

Lydia must have realized he didn't understand what she wanted, so she stood up and walked over to the sofa and invited him to follow. She rose to her toes to kiss him and started unbuttoning his shirt, causing him to freeze and grab her hands.

"Lydia?" he whispered, looking into her eyes as he swallowed hard, understanding now. "Are you… do you…can we? I don't want to hurt the baby."

Lydia smiled at him, her eyes gleaming. "Henry…" She chuckled. "It won't hurt the baby."

"Are you sure?" Henry released her hands, and she continued unbuttoning his shirt.

"Yes." She looked into his eyes as she pushed his shirt off his shoulders before her hands reached for his belt.

Chapter 7

Making New Friends

Three weeks later, Henry was back in the Cayman Islands at Philip's estate. He hated leaving Lydia because she was having a difficult time with morning sickness. He knew there wasn't much he could do to help, but he wanted to be there for her as much as he could.

The lawyer, George Magee, met him at the airport and drove him to the estate. The place was locked up tight. He knew Lydia had released all the staff, but he wasn't prepared for how deserted the place would be. To his surprise, it had remained undisturbed these past several weeks since she left.

George Magee unlocked the front door, and they went inside the house. Henry showed George a copy of the appraisal that he had provided to Philip and pointed out the pieces that he advised should be sold prior to the donation of the collection. George slid on a pair of reading glasses and studied the list. "I see. Yes, Ms. Casper told me you would recommend the sale of a few items. Good then. It will take me a couple of days to get the paperwork drafted and another day to arrange the transport of the art to London and then to the National Gallery or auction house."

"Fair enough, George. I'll start packaging and labeling the art for shipment." Through Lydia, he had let George know in advance what supplies he needed, and he found it all ready for him in the great room of the house. He spent the rest of the day packaging the art and estimated that he was about halfway through the list. Time had gotten away from him and he realized it was probably too late to call Lydia, but he tried anyway.

"Hullo?" she answered, sounding half asleep.

"It's me," he said. "I'm sorry to call so late...I lost track of time."

Lydia yawned into the phone. "I don't mind, darling. Is everything going alright?"

"Everything is fine here. How was your day?" he asked, smiling into the phone.

"Oh...bog-standard," she mumbled drowsily.

Henry grinned. He'd never heard her use that expression before. "How are you feeling?"

"I was sick three times today before lunch, but better in the afternoon." Her voice was faint, as if she was barely holding the phone properly.

"I'm sorry, Lydia. When we see your midwife next week, maybe she'll be able to help." Henry felt badly for her and truly hoped she could get some relief soon. He was both excited and nervous about the visit to see the midwife; the newness of all of this kept him on his toes.

"I hope so," she murmured and yawned into the phone again.

"Go back to sleep. I'm sorry I woke you," he said sheepishly. "I promise to call at a better time tomorrow."

"Alright, darling. I love you. Goodnight," she replied sleepily.

Henry blinked and took a moment to register what she had said. She hadn't said *"I love you"* before...but as soon as he heard her say it, he knew. "I love you too, Lydia. Goodnight." He held the phone to his ear until she hung up.

He felt lighter than air as he walked into the office, finding George, who also appeared to be reaching a stopping point for his task. "Making progress?" Henry asked with a smile.

"Indeed, I am. But now, I'm ready for dinner. Let's close up shop, shall we?" George responded, looking up at Henry over his reading glasses. They shut off all the lights and secured the doors to the house before leaving. George drove Henry to his hotel and, after checking into his room, grabbed dinner in the hotel restaurant.

The next morning, George picked him up at around 10:00 a.m. and they returned to Philip's house, picking up where they left off. Henry plugged in an electric clock in a spot where he could easily watch the time. He wanted to call Lydia at 7:00 p.m. in London, so he did the math and resolved to break at the appropriate time. He wondered if she would remember talking to him last night.

Henry had just finished packaging the largest piece in the collection when his eyes drifted up to the clock and saw that it was almost fifteen minutes after the time to call Lydia. Pulling the gloves off of his hands, he went straight to the telephone. He dialed her number and it rang a few times, but her answering machine picked up. He left a message, saying that he would try again in an hour.

As soon as he hung up, he heard a loud commotion at the front of the house. There were multiple voices shouting in what sounded like Afrikaans, and he rushed to the office where George was working. George looked terrified, gaping out the window. "George!" Henry whispered. "What's happening?"

"I don't know, Henry; I don't know!"

"Take the papers and hide; get under the desk," Henry urged George, then gingerly stepped into the hallway, uncertain about what was going to happen. He swallowed his fear and drew himself to his full height before walking toward the shouting.

At the front of the house were three armed men wearing black fatigues, having a heated discussion in Afrikaans. Henry noticed their weapons and raised his hands in submission. "Can I help you?" he asked confidently, trying to put on a brave face.

The three men looked at him and the man in the middle—tall with a medium build, dark hair, and sun-kissed light-ochre skin—approached Henry, pulling his gun out of the holster and waving it in his face. "Who the hell are you?"

"Henry. Who are you?" he responded.

The man pressed the gun into Henry's chest while laughing. "I'm the man who's going to shoot you if you don't do what I say."

"Understood. Tell me what you need."

The man laughed again and looked over his shoulder at the two men he was with. "Where's the Indian girl?"

Henry felt panic spreading through his chest, knowing the man was referring to Lydia. He weighed the pros and cons of playing dumb as his eyes dropped to the gun. "She's not here anymore. When Philip died, the staff were all let go."

The man pistol-whipped Henry across the face. "Let me remind you I'll shoot you if you don't give me what I want."

Henry doubled over and held his face. He felt a gash under his right eye, then pulled a trembling hand away, which was covered in blood. Steeling himself, he stood upright. "You asked me where she was, and I told you what I know. If you're going to shoot me, then shoot me." Henry felt his adrenaline take over, and he was no longer afraid.

"My brother and his associates were here weeks ago, and he told me an Indian servant girl said she could help move our poppies. But I haven't heard from my brother since and our poppies haven't been moved." The man snarled with intense agitation.

Henry knew the man's brother was dead, but he didn't see how telling him that would improve his situation, and he didn't know what else to say.

"You know what I think?" the man continued, putting the gun in Henry's face again. "I think you know who she is."

Henry maintained unwavering eye contact. "I only met her once. Maybe she went back to India," he lied expertly.

"Nooo," the man said, drawing out the word, shaking his head. "There was a rumor that Philip had a daughter that lived in London, but no one had ever seen her...at least they thought they hadn't. I've been here dozens of times to meet with Philip...sometimes there's an Indian servant girl attending to him, and sometimes there isn't." The man put his gun back in the holster. "She was beautiful, so I assumed she was his mistress, but looking back, I don't recall any evidence of that kind of relationship." The man's eyes dug into Henry's soul, and Henry fought hard to not betray anything through the fear he was feeling again. "When my brother told me Philip was dead and the only one who would talk to him was the Indian servant girl, the pieces fell into place." He paused, almost as if for effect. "She's his daughter, isn't she?" The man smiled, but it was not a pleasant smile; it was a smile of victory...of a snake who had cornered his rodent prey and was ready to strike. "Say nothing if I'm right."

Henry's voice burst from his throat abruptly. "You're wrong. Philip had no children." It was technically true and false at the same time, but he knew he had to say something to try to re-direct the man's suspicions.

"That was an even better confirmation than silence." The man pulled a cigar and a lighter out of his pocket, put the cigar in his mouth and lit it, taking several long draws before blowing the smoke into Henry's face. "Who is she to you?"

Henry said nothing, hating the fact that this man had deduced as much as he had, unsure of what he could say to make it better.

"Here's what's going to happen: I don't care how you do it, but you are going to arrange for my poppies to get moved; do you hear me? And I won't leave until it's done. When you make the arrangements, you can then return to whatever the hell you were doing...but not before you do what Philip promised."

Henry felt lightheaded. The blood draining from the cut on his face soaked his shirt. He opened his mouth to protest, not knowing the first thing about arranging for the movement of poppies.

"If you don't do what I want, I'll kill you and then I'll go to London and will tear the place apart until I find her, and then I'll kill her...but not before I *taste* her, do you understand me?"

Henry felt sick to his stomach upon hearing the man's words. His black eyes laughed as he took a long drag on the cigar held between his smiling yellow teeth. Henry nodded.

Lydia had told Henry her father's book of contacts was in a lockbox at his bank. Henry needed that book. He returned to the office where George was and approached his hiding place. "George," he said, then glanced at the smoking man. "George, I need access to Phillip's lockbox."

George peeped his head out from under the desk and his eyes locked onto the cut on Henry's cheek and his blood-soaked shirt. "The lockbox?" he repeated dumbly.

"Yes, George. The lockbox. At the bank. This is quite urgent." Henry's eyes were intense and pleading that George would snap to it.

George then looked at the man in black and stood up. "Right. Shall I drive, then?"

George drove the three of them to Philip's bank, stopping at Henry's hotel first so he could change his shirt and clean his face.

At the bank, Henry and George walked inside with the ever-present shadow trailing behind them. Only George could access the lockbox, so Henry told him there was a brown leather book that he needed.

"A book?" George asked, drawing together his eyebrows. "I'm not aware of a book in the lockbox."

"I'm certain it's there," Henry insisted. Lydia must have put it in the lockbox without George's knowledge.

George nodded, looking skeptical, and was escorted to the vault by a bank worker.

Henry waited in silence with his hands in his pockets, periodically glancing at the man in black. Several minutes later, George returned holding a brown leather book in his hand. "Well, you were right, Henry. Here's the book," George said. "It must have been placed there by Lyd—"

"Thank you, George. We should go." Henry quickly cut him off before he could say Lydia's name.

During the drive back to the house, Henry flipped through the book, focusing on the specialties written next to the names within.

"Where do you need the poppies moved to?" He remembered Lydia said Burma, but he wanted to hold his cards close to the chest.

"Burma...or Myanmar...whatever the fuck they call it these days," the man in black grumbled.

Henry found "Middle Eastern Ground Transport" next to the name Ibrahim Al Ahmed. He lived in Pakistan.

Back at the house, Henry marched into Philip's office and told the man in black to give him all the details: the exact location of the poppy field, the name of the contact at the poppy field, who will receive the shipment in Burma, and the location in Burma.

"And what about payment? No one will move this stuff for free," Henry boldly proclaimed.

"Philip and I agreed on a price. I'll honor it," the man said.

Henry hesitated. He wasn't expecting that response, but of course it made sense. Philip made money by arranging these kinds of transactions.

"It's up to you how much you pay the ones who do the work; that's not my problem," the man in black elaborated.

Henry scratched his cheek, feeling uneasy. He peered at George, who was keeping quiet. He really didn't want to get involved in this, but the man in black wasn't giving him other options. After taking a deep breath, he picked up the phone, dialing the phone number for Ibrahim Al Ahmed. He answered the phone and Henry asked if he spoke English, and he did. Henry then explained that he was an associate of Philip

Casper's, and he had a job for him. Ibrahim asked for the details, which Henry relayed. Ibrahim then became more enthusiastic, saying that he had talked to Philip about this job briefly a few months ago. He said he was ready to execute on his word.

"But first, let's discuss price. I'll do this job for... fifty percent," Ibrahim said.

Henry honestly didn't know what the cut should be, but something possessed him to push back. "No. Thirty-five percent."

Ibrahim was silent for a long moment and George and the man in black watched him with neutral expressions.

"Forty percent," Ibrahim countered.

"Thirty-eight percent. That's the highest I'll go," Henry concluded firmly.

After a brief pause, Ibrahim started laughing. "You bargain just like Philip. Where is he anyway?"

Henry glanced at George again. "He retired."

"I understand," Ibrahim said, and Henry wondered if he really did, or if he just thought he did. Either way, he wasn't sure it was a good idea to broadcast the fact that Philip was dead right at that moment.

"I will do this by the end of the week. I look forward to seeing the money in my account," Ibrahim said jovially.

"I assume the account is the same?" Henry asked, then read out the number in the book.

"You have it, Henry," Ibrahim said with his thick accent. "I'll call from Burma. Or is it Myanmar now?" Ibrahim said, adding a laugh.

Henry felt relieved, and he looked up at the man in black. "I appreciate the urgency, Ibrahim. Please call when it's done." Henry hung up and thought he might vomit, explaining that it would be done this week.

The man in black grinned and pulled another cigar out of his pocket. "Appreciate the urgency, indeed," he said, putting the cigar between his teeth. "I'll be back Friday. Well done, Henry." The man stood and left the office. Henry leaned back in the chair, feeling defeated, and flinched when he heard the front door slam shut. He looked at the time; it was 4:30 p.m. He cussed and picked up the phone, calling Lydia again...assuming he missed her call-back while they were at the bank. He asked George to give him a few minutes, who got up and left.

"Hullo?" she answered.

"Lydia. Thank God," Henry said, relieved to get a hold of her. It made him uneasy to know that her secret identity was not as secret as they thought. "Did you get my message earlier?"

"I did; I'm sorry I missed your call. I was trying to wrap up a project at work and I stayed a bit later than usual."

Henry exhaled and the tension of the day melted away as she spoke. "Are you feeling better today?"

"Actually, I am," she replied, and he could hear a smile in her voice. "How are things going with George?"

Henry contemplated whether to tell her about the return of the drug dealers; he didn't want her to worry, but he also didn't feel comfortable withholding it from her. "Listen...something happened today..." he said, deciding that it would be better for her to know...he didn't want to keep secrets from her. He described the events, starting with the intrusion of the men, through his phone call with Ibrahim. Lydia was appalled.

"This is why I wanted to let the place rot. Papa was far too accommodating with his bloody clients."

Henry felt like it was all his fault. It was his suggestion to sell the art. "I'm sorry. This happened because of me."

Lydia sighed. "No, Henry. This happened because the world is full of cruel and greedy men. The sooner you get back here, the sooner we can put all this behind us."

Henry agreed with her. "Yes; I'm ready to come back...but I still have a lot of art to package up." He remembered the pieces set up in the great room that he was working on. "Oh...and, again, I apologize for calling you so late last night. I hope you could get back to sleep."

"Did you like the way we ended the call?" Lydia chuckled.

He laughed and stared at his hands. "I did. You caught me by surprise."

"Nothing quite like exhaustion to bring out the truth," she said.

Henry wished he could touch her right now. "I do love you, Lydia...I think I've loved you since you recited that French poem here on the beach."

"A strange twist of fate brought us together, didn't it? As hard as I tried to distance myself from my father's affairs, it was that which ultimately led me to you."

"You're right. What are the odds that we meet on the beach, share an amazing night, and then meet again the next day at a place neither of us expected to see the other? I think you could call that fate."

She laughed. "Do you believe in fate, Henry?"

He closed his eyes and pictured her face, and he remembered how scared she was when she told him she was pregnant. "I do, Lydia."

She didn't speak for a long moment. "I miss you, darling."

"I miss you, too."

"I'm going to get ready for bed; will you call me tomorrow?"

"I will. Sleep well," he said. "I love you." He felt warmth spread through his chest after the words left his mouth.

"I love you, too, darling. Goodnight." She hung up.

Henry put the phone down and stood up from the desk. "George?" A moment later, George returned to the office, putting his glasses on his face. "Let's get back to work."

George looked at Henry. "You handled that situation very well."

With a sigh and a furrowed brow, Henry replied, "Well, I didn't have an option for it to be anything but successful."

"You negotiated a nice profit for yourself. Philip would have been pleased."

Henry shook his head. "None of that money is mine. I don't want it."

"Well..." George took a seat at the desk and spread out the paperwork that he was working on earlier. "Then you negotiated a nice profit for Ms. Casper."

"She doesn't want it either. The only money she wants is the proceeds from the sale of the art we are arranging."

George peered up at Henry. "Whether she wants it or not, that money is hers."

"I think she would have a lot to say about that."

"Perhaps. But if she won't talk to me and tell me what to do, I'll have to proceed with transferring everything to her name."

Henry thought about the implications of this and shook his head. "Please don't do that...she's already at risk of exposure. Philip tried to shield her from this life; putting everything in her name would thrust her headfirst into it."

"I understand, but Philip's will is quite clear that everything should go to her."

Henry cussed and put his hands on his hips. "I'll talk to her, okay?" He turned to leave, but remembered something he needed to say to George. "I'm glad you're here, George; I wouldn't have been able to get rid of our cigar smoking friend without your help, but...please don't allude to Lydia's existence around him...or anyone else... again."

George looked sheepish. "Of course. It won't happen again."

Henry nodded. "Thank you."

CHAPTER 8

CHALLENGE ACCEPTED

Wednesday and Thursday passed uneventfully. George completed the paperwork for the art donation and sales. Henry scrutinized it, making sure it was accurate. Henry also finished packaging the rest of the paintings.

Thursday afternoon, Henry convinced Lydia to speak to George about her father's will. She confirmed to George that she didn't want her name on anything that belonged to her father, except for the new account that should be set up to receive the proceeds from the sale of the art. George suggested putting the assets into an anonymous trust. Lydia agreed and instructed George to put her and Henry on the trust as the controlling parties. Henry asked her if she was sure she wanted him on the trust, and she said that she was. "As the father of my child, I foresee that we have a long future together. Also, your practicality is the yin to my impulsive, emotional yang. We'll work together to decide on how to dispose of my father's business."

George said he would take care of everything and offered his congratulations. "Starting a family is both exciting and scary. I wish you both the best!"

They thanked George, and he excused himself so that he could get started on the paperwork for the trust. Henry and Lydia talked for a few more minutes, discussing plans to spend a weekend in the highlands of Scotland when he returned.

Friday morning came, and Henry was nervous about the return of the man in black. He also hoped that Ibrahim was successful in his task, so that he could be done with this once and for all. George picked him up from his hotel and told him he had finished all the paperwork for the trust and the new bank account. He told Henry that he needed his signature on the documents as the co-owner since Lydia wasn't there, then he could file them and make the transfer official. Henry said they could take care of it first thing that morning.

They pulled up in front of the house and the man in black was waiting there already, smoking a cigar and leaning against his Land Rover. Henry cussed and touched the cut under his eye. "Guess I shouldn't be surprised."

George nodded. "This will all be done with soon enough, Henry."

They parked the car and Henry and George went to the front door, promptly joined by the man in black. George held his briefcase tightly against his body as he unlocked the door.

"Good morning, gentlemen," the man said, a cloud of smoke hovering around his face as he spoke.

Henry nodded in acknowledgment as George opened the door. They stood in the foyer and Henry invited the man to make himself comfortable in the parlor while he and George took care of some business.

"I'll gladly stay away if you have some whiskey to keep me company."

Henry remembered Philip's liquor cabinet in his office. "Of course; give me a moment."

George and Henry walked to the office and as George took a seat at the desk, Henry opened the cabinet where Philip had retrieved the cognac and found a barely opened bottle of Jameson. He took the bottle to the man and told him to enjoy it.

When Henry returned to the office, George had an impressive amount of paperwork arranged in neat piles on the desk.

"Good God, George. Did you spend all night pulling this together?"

George grinned. "Not quite; most of this has been prepared for weeks and has been ready to attach to the official paperwork."

Henry suddenly felt a lot more nervous about all of this; George must have picked up on it.

"Philip was a very successful man and the nature of his business forced him to diversify his assets. If and when you and Ms. Casper decide to liquidate any of this, I can certainly assist. Try not to feel overwhelmed."

Henry nodded and sat down opposite George as he explained what everything was. Philip had multiple accounts holding a variety of investments; cars, antiques, a freighter ship, a sailboat, this estate in the Cayman Islands, and many other things. George asked Henry to sign in a few places here and there, explaining what the signature was communicating. George flipped to the front page of the package and asked for a final signature.

Henry skimmed over the page, but the blood drained from his face when he read the summary. The total value of the assets being transferred into the trust was about two-hundred million pounds. He stood up abruptly and returned to the liquor cabinet and poured himself a generous glass of scotch.

George peered at him over his glasses. "Are you alright, Henry?"

Henry took a long drink, glancing at George sideways. He picked the pen back up and quickly scribbled his name for the final signature.

"Henry?" George repeated.

He set the pen back down and ran a hand through his hair. "I just need a minute, George." Henry's brain shifted into high gear. He'd never been exposed to so much money in his life. He took another long drink of the scotch, trying to silence the voice in his head that was rejoicing over his sudden increase in wealth. *This is not my money...this money is dirty...earned illegally,* he thought in response.

The phone rang and forced Henry out of his inner conflict. He picked up the phone. "Hello?"

"This is Ibrahim. Henry?"

"Yes, Ibrahim. Is it done?"

"It is done." He offered to put the Burmese poppy processor on the phone and Henry thought it wouldn't hurt. He asked George to fetch the man in black so he would have his confirmation.

Moments later, George returned with the man, and Henry handed him the phone. After a brief exchange where he clearly confirmed that his poppies were delivered, he handed the phone back to Henry, who closed with Ibrahim, saying that the money transfer would be initiated today. He hung up and peered at the man in black with narrowed eyes. "I think our business is almost complete. Do you need to call your bank?" Henry took another sip of his drink.

"I suppose I do," he responded.

Henry glanced at George. "Give him the account information, please." Henry stood and stared out the window, putting his hands in his pockets, trying to compartmentalize his thoughts and feelings. He wished Lydia were there.

He could hear George and the man in black behind him on the phone and the exchanging of numbers and he also heard George having a separate, one-sided conversation. Henry was so tuned out at the moment that he didn't realize that the man in black was addressing him.

"*Eish*! Earth to Henry." The man got into Henry's ear to get his attention.

Henry snapped out of his daze and turned his head to face him, bearing an expression that was fully intended to communicate that he didn't like the man.

"You did good, Henry. To quote Bogie, I think this is the beginning of a beautiful friendship."

Henry drained the last of his scotch and set the glass down firmly. "No. This is the first and last time I'll be helping you...you'll have to find someone else to facilitate your drug business."

The man glared at him. "You must be crazy. Don't you remember what I said? Do I need to get on the next plane to London, Henry?"

Henry assumed the man wasn't wearing his gun today because he didn't see it and the man hadn't pulled it on him, but he didn't rule out other weapons that might be a little more discreet. Henry took a wide step to face him and create a little more space. "If you show your face in London, I'll kill you myself." Henry was furious that the man was using Lydia as a pawn.

The man in black stared at Henry for a long moment. "I believe you." He took another cigar out of his pocket, put it in his mouth, and lit it. "Have you ever been on safari, Henry?"

Henry furrowed his brow. "No."

"I used to take rich tourists on week-long safaris on the African savannah. You should go sometime; it's a life-changing experience." The man took a long drag on the cigar. "One day, we came upon a pride of lions, but there was quite the commotion happening. You see, a pride of lions is largely female, with only a handful of sexually mature males. Usually, as male cubs come of age, they are driven out of the pride if they don't leave on their own. Sometimes if a ruling male of the pride is getting too old, a younger male might challenge him to take his place." As the man spoke, the smoke he inhaled from his cigar slowly drifted out of his mouth and nostrils, making him look like an odd, personified caricature of a bull. "This young lion challenged the old lion, but the old lion," the man wagged his finger at Henry, "wasn't ready to give up his place in the pride. Those lionesses belonged to him." He sucked on his cigar. "From where we observed this intense clash, I could see the fire in the eyes of the old lion. He was prepared to kill to protect his mating rights, and he did." The man took the cigar out of his mouth. "I see that same fire in your eyes, Henry."

Henry swallowed hard and set his jaw. "You should go."

The man nodded and turned away. "My brother is dead, isn't he?" He glanced at Henry over his shoulder.

Henry considered how to respond. "He shouldn't have threatened her." He was nervous about making the declaration because, in reality, he had absolutely nothing to do with the termination of the man's brother, but maybe if he believed Henry did, it might add a little more weight to his earlier statement. Of course, there was the other possibility that the man would want revenge for the death of his brother.

The man's face transformed with a grin. "He was an idiot, anyway. More money for me." He put the cigar back in his mouth. "You're a natural at this, Henry. I'm certain our paths will cross again. And your lovely lioness is safe...she'll come to no harm from me."

Henry dropped his eyes for a moment, feeling an odd mixture of shame and triumph.

"You know...you asked who I was, and I never told you." The man turned one more time to face Henry, who merely glared back at him with a stone face. "Jaku Van Der Meer."

Henry nodded. "Goodbye, Jaku."

"Farewell, Henry."

CHAPTER 9

PLAYING WITH FIRE

Several months passed, and Henry and Lydia were eagerly awaiting the arrival of their baby. Henry had moved into Lydia's flat shortly after he returned from the Island and they got married in a simple ceremony in New York so Geoffrey, Henry's father, could attend. The art pieces did exceptionally well at auction, and they had a very nice nest egg set aside for the baby.

Since establishing the trust, they started slowly selling off Philip's assets, namely his sailboat, cars, and some antiques. The sales were relatively easy, and George helped them take care of it from the island. They also hired a small security team to keep watch at the house, especially since George had been there helping with sorting out things to prepare to sell. They didn't want to risk him getting into a dangerous situation while helping them.

The day finally came that Lydia gave birth to a healthy baby boy. They were both immediately in love with him and they named him Geoffrey

Thomas Coats. He had Lydia's eyes and mouth, but Henry's skin tone and nose. They were on Cloud Nine, falling into this new routine effortlessly, considering the pregnancy was unplanned.

The months passed and life was good. Henry earned a promotion at the National Gallery and Lydia got a new role with the Ministry of Defense. They had a nanny that they adored and who adored baby Geoffrey in return.

One day, George called Lydia and Henry and told them that there was a man who was interested in buying the estate. "Have you considered selling the property here?" George asked as they both listened.

Lydia turned to Henry. "Eventually we wanted to sell it, but maybe we should go ahead and do it if there's a serious buyer interested." Henry nodded in agreement as Lydia relayed the message to George.

George explained it would probably be best for one or both of them to come down to meet the buyer and make sure they were comfortable with the situation and to be involved in any price negotiations.

After a brief discussion, Henry and Lydia agreed that Henry would go alone; he wanted to ensure that Lydia could keep her distance from the place, remembering how Jaku had connected the dots of who she was. What if others had done the same? He told George that he would plan on being there in three weeks.

The day came for him to fly to the Islands. Lydia and Baby Geoffrey accompanied Henry to the airport and had a warm farewell at the gate. He kissed her tenderly and gave his son a squeeze before getting on the plane. Hours later, he was driving to the estate in a rented Range Rover. He parked and was greeted expertly by Davis, the leader of the security team they had hired. They'd never met in person before but had spoken on the phone several times. George was waiting in the study and greeted Henry jovially.

"Welcome back, Henry! I hope your flight was comfortable."

"Thank you, George! It was just fine...a long trip. Glad to be on the ground again. So what's new?"

George updated Henry on island events. Since he was here last, half a dozen, or so, of Philip's clients dropped by looking for his assistance. The security team provided him with much comfort during these visits, as some of them were not pleased at being turned away.

Henry shook his head. "Getting rid of this place will save us these headaches, but I pity the next owners...I hope they are thick-skinned."

"Well, funny you should mention that; the one who wants to buy it is one of Philip's clients."

"Oh really? Well...that should create an interesting dynamic."

George nodded. "Indeed! I have arranged dinner for us to meet and talk tonight."

Since Henry was on the island on his own dime, he opted to stay at the estate instead of a hotel. He stayed in the room that had been Lydia's when she would visit. He unpacked his suitcase and called Lydia to let her know he made it. They talked until Geoffrey woke from a nap, then hung up so Lydia could nurse him.

Henry took a walk around the estate outside, enjoying the sunshine and breeze, a vast difference from the dreary climate of London.

It was nearing dinner time and Henry learned they would have dinner at the estate and a private chef would prepare it. He changed into proper dinner attire and waited in the parlor, drinking a small amount of bourbon and reading a book. It was 7:30 p.m. when Henry heard a knock at the door. He left the parlor and waited in the foyer as Davis answered it.

He could hear a brief exchange between Davis and the man at the door. Davis knew they were expecting someone, so he was likely vetting him to confirm he was the one they were waiting for. A moment later, Davis escorted the man inside. They approached Henry while George stepped into the foyer.

"Ah! Excellent timing," George said. "Henry this is Dmitri Ivanov. Mr. Ivanov, this is Henry Coats."

Henry smiled in greeting, but was feeling uncertain, having his previous experience with Jaku. He extended a hand, which Dmitri took.

"Henry Coats! Pleasure to meet you," he said happily, with a thick Russian accent. "I am so glad Philip has good help sorting out his business. I was very sad to hear that he died; he was good friend. I've known him many years."

Henry glanced at George, surprised; *George said this man was a client, right?* "A pleasure to meet you, as well. Pardon my surprise, but I thought you were one of Philip's clients."

"I was! But I was his friend before I was his client."

Henry kept eye contact with Dmitri. He had a cheerful face and a contagious smile. "I see. Do you mind if I ask what Philip did for you? His services were so varied; it helps me to understand his business even better."

"Not at all. My cousin, Evgene, operates a very successful *wodka* distillery in Moscow. Philip helped us distribute the product to our customers all over the world." Dmitri winked at Henry. "I know what you're thinking...how much of that *wodka* was illegally distributed? And I promise you, it was all perfectly legal. I know Philip struggled with shaking loose some of his more... distasteful clients...but our business was clean."

They walked to the dining room where dinner was waiting, and Henry and Dmitri then fell into a pleasant conversation about Moscow. Henry even reverted to speaking Russian a few times as he reminisced about the years he spent there as a boy, and Dmitri was overjoyed that Henry could speak the language.

After dinner, the three of them retreated to the office and Henry offered to pour a round of drinks for all of them. They decided collectively that vodka would be a proper digestif and Henry obliged with a brand-new bottle.

They all took a seat and Henry was prepared to pivot the discussion to the sale of the estate when Dmitri asked about Lydia. Henry stared at George with an accusation in his eyes, but George shook his head, communicating that he said nothing about her. When neither Henry nor George responded, Dmitri elaborated. "I did not intend to catch you off guard. I know Philip went to extreme measures to guard her. I knew her as a child... before Philip was forced to change her name, though she probably wouldn't remember me. I had heard from a mutual friend that she was here after Philip died. Are either of you in touch with her?"

Henry cleared his throat. "Well, yes. But...do you mind if I ask about this mutual friend and how he learned she was here?"

"She called him asking for help. I understand that some of Philip's more unsavory clients were here beating their chests like gorillas." Dmitri shook his head. "She must have been terrified."

Henry wanted to ask who the friend was, in case he ever got the opportunity to thank him, but Dmitri continued.

"Lydia was a lovely girl; just a year younger than my daughter. Philip was so proud of her." Dmitri sipped on his vodka and Henry softened toward him.

"Actually, Lydia is my wife. We met here, shortly before Philip died."

"Oh! So you are newlywed? *Pozdravleniya*! Congratulations! I am happy for you both."

Henry smiled at Dmitri. "Thank you." Henry glanced at George, who looked relaxed as he drank his vodka. "So, Dmitri, I understand you are interested in buying this property. Do you have questions for us, or any concerns that we can discuss?"

"Actually, I have slight confession to make. I do not want to buy the property. But I did hope to convince you to carry on the business." Dmitri set his glass down and leaned toward Henry with an apologetic posture.

"Oh…" Henry furrowed his brow, feeling perturbed by the confession. He would have been a lot more upset if he didn't like Dmitri so much. "I see. Well…the problem with continuing the business comes with so many things: location, clientele—present company excluded— reputation…I studied art at university and that is the career that I've built in London. I'm not confident I would be effective at running this business, even if the clientele were all law-abiding citizens."

"But you see! You would have the power to clean house! Do what Philip could not and clean up the client base. The risk of this business is far more palatable when you aren't in danger of being hounded by INTERPOL."

Henry leaned back in his chair, studying Dmitri. "Then there's Lydia. She wants no part of it, either. From her perspective, her father's business ruined his life and placed a heavy burden on her and her mother. Even if I wanted to pursue the business, it would be a rather selfish request of Lydia. I couldn't do that to her."

"I understand the dilemma...but all I am asking is that you think about it. This business could make you very wealthy man...even when everything is, as they say, above board."

Henry was ashamed that the idea of the money was appealing. He grew up very wealthy and, while his father now supplemented him regularly, he was embarrassed that it was necessary. He should be able to take care of his family himself through money he earned, without needing to be subsidized by his father's wealth. The proceeds from the sale of the art helped with baby Geoffrey, but he wished it hadn't been necessary.

"Look...Dmitri, I appreciate your confidence, but as I said, I wouldn't know the first thing about running a business like this."

"It can't be all that different from arranging the movement of millions worth of art." He took another sip of vodka and grinned at Henry. "A little birdy told me that a new lot of art was donated anonymously to the National Gallery in London, but this birdy swears they had seen some of these pieces at Philip's estate in the Cayman Islands."

Henry regarded the vodka in his glass. He glanced at George, whose expression seemed to reflect a person observing the volleys of a tennis match. Henry suspected why Dmitri was so interested in the continuation of the business. "Dmitri...do you have a vodka shipment that needs to be moved?"

The Russian looked sheepish, running a finger around the rim of his glass. "How did you guess?"

Henry chuckled. "Look...I'll do this for you, Dmitri. Since you were a friend of Philip's, I think Lydia will understand wanting to help you out."

Dmitri clapped his hands together and muttered something in Russian, an expression that communicated relief. "Thank you, Henry! Thank you! You have saved me great, big headache."

They discussed the details of the vodka shipment, and Henry checked Philip's book to see if he could locate someone who could assist. They had a couple more rounds of vodka as Henry made some calls to arrange the shipment from Moscow to Norway. By the time they finished the third round, the shipment was arranged, and Dmitri was calling his bank to request a wire transfer to the trust bank account. Dmitri asked Henry how much he owed him, and Henry was torn. He had no idea what the service was worth, but also...he worried about how Lydia would feel about it.

"What did you normally pay Philip?" Henry asked.

"For a shipment this size, about 300,000 pounds."

Henry looked at George, who nodded. "Sounds fair to me." Henry grinned at Dmitri as he drank the last of his vodka. They concluded the business and retired to the cabana, where Dmitri lit a cigar. His manners with the cigar were much better than Jaku's. He offered one to Henry and George, but both declined.

They spent another hour or so talking. Henry learned Dmitri met Philip in Vietnam. At the time, Philip had a position with MI6, and they tasked him with observing up close what was happening in Vietnam. Though the UK was not involved in the Vietnam conflict, they clearly felt it prudent to stay informed of how things were evolving. Dmitri was placed there by the KGB to pose as a sympathizer and misdirect US intelligence officers regarding the spread of communism, as facilitated by the Soviet Union, but he ended up being turned into an asset for the US, a fact that Mother Russia—to this day—had no knowledge of. In the process, Philip and Dmitri struck up an unlikely friendship, along with the American that turned him.

Dmitri told interesting stories, often referring to his American contact, but seemed to be careful about not stating his name. Henry was curious why that was, but opted to mind his business and not dig into it. Dmitri was so forthcoming about other details that he figured he would have been explicit if he could.

Henry learned that Dmitri's duplicity was successful, however, and he was granted diplomatic rights by Russia in recognition for his "service". He and Philip were able to further nurture their friendship when Philip was ultimately given diplomat status by the English Crown.

Eventually, Dmitri left and Henry went to bed. The next day, he arose at his leisure and planned to arrange his departure back to London. He thought about the events last night, amazed at how easy it was to arrange the shipment for Dmitri...the easiest money he'd ever made. His mind examined the possibility of taking Dmitri's advice and continuing on with the business, but only with the "clean" clients. The more he thought about it, the more appealing it was. He wanted to talk to Lydia about it but thought it would be more appropriate to have the discussion in person. He called Lydia to let her know they wrapped up the business quickly, so he was coming home already.

"Did we sell the estate?" she asked with anticipation in her voice.

"No; I'll explain when I'm home. I love you. See you soon," he said, ending the call.

The next day, he was back in London. His flight landed after 9:00 p.m., so he took a black cab to their flat from the airport. Lydia was lounging on the sofa, reading a magazine, when Henry walked through the door.

"Hullo, Darling." She smiled and moved to stand.

"No, no; don't get up." He left his suitcase by the door as he took a seat on the sofa next to her. They exchanged a sweet kiss, and she asked how his flight was. He let her know it was just fine and asked how Geoffrey was, and she informed him he was perfect; the best baby on the planet, she said with a smile.

"So, what happened to the potential buyer?"

Henry paused a moment, trying to think of the best way to tee this up. He decided in the end that a chronological play-by-play was the best way to approach it. He talked through the events of the meeting with Dmitri, staying tuned into any shifts in her demeanor; staying aware of places where he might need to stop and give her a chance to speak. He finished the story and studied her face. He noticed how tired her eyes were.

She shifted in her seat. "Henry, darling..." she started. "It's easy to say you could clean up the client list, but," she took one of his hands, "some of Papa's clients are very dangerous men. Getting rid of them won't be that simple. I don't want you to get caught in that trap...just like my father did."

Henry kissed her hand. "It may not be simple, but it's not impossible. I have an idea of how to tempt them to find someone else to take care of their dirty business."

Lydia sighed and leaned against him. "Henry..."

He kissed her head and could smell her hair; she smelled like roses. "I understand, Lydia. I'd never do anything that makes you uncomfortable."

She pulled her head back and looked into his face for a long moment. "Darling, if you really want to do this...I support you."

It took him a moment to understand that she was saying yes. He locked his eyes on hers. "Are you sure? Please don't feel pressured."

She touched his cheek. "I don't feel pressured. I believe in you, Henry."

"I love you, Lydia. I want to take care of our family. I even want to cleanse the business of the dirty money."

"How do you plan to do that?" she asked with a raised eyebrow.

"Well...how much of your father's income was from illegal transactions? If you had to guess?"

"Oh...40%...if I had to guess."

Henry nodded. "Alright. Then 40% of the cash in the trust bank account will be reserved and donated to any causes you choose."

"Really?" Her face brightened. "I love that idea!" she said with gleaming eyes.

"I already discussed it with George and he's ready to make it official on your word."

Lydia crawled onto his lap and kissed him deeply; a kiss that communicated her appreciation and love for him...and something else, too. "Let's go to the bedroom," she whispered after the kiss, and he quickly obliged.

CHAPTER 10

A PART TO PLAY

The months passed and George had set aside the charity fund. Their first donation was for one million pounds to the orphanage Lydia had been adopted from. The donation was anonymous, of course, but it made the news on the BBC.

Henry flew down to the islands periodically to meet with George and discuss the business. While there, he could learn more about the mechanics of the business, including things that George had exclusively handled up to this point, like banking and bookkeeping. So far, they were successful at turning away the bad clients that had surfaced. A combination of the increased security team onsite, plus some financial incentive, tempted them to seek help elsewhere.

Baby Geoffrey's first birthday came and went and they had just returned to London from visiting Henry's father in New York when George called. He was frantic and explained to Henry that another of Philip's criminal clients had shown up, but he wasn't taking no for an answer. Henry learned the security team was forced to physically remove the man, but he feared that it only caused the animosity to escalate. He believed it was only a matter of time before the criminal would return. Henry ran a hand through his hair and listened, not sure what to do. Henry confirmed George offered the man money to cover his trouble; George explained that he even tried to double the amount, but the man would not be moved. He asked George what specifically the man needed.

"He's sold uranium to Iran; he needs it delivered to them."

All the air left the room when Henry heard "uranium". He cussed under his breath. Lydia was busy corralling Geoffrey in the nursery while she unpacked their suitcases, so she had heard none of this conversation. Henry didn't want to worry her, so he hoped to keep this quiet. He told George to instruct the security team lead to recruit more men and he would get back in contact with him as soon as possible. He hung up and joined Lydia in the nursery, intending to call Dmitri later to see if he had any advice for him.

Later that evening, while Lydia was taking a bubble bath—inspired by Henry's suggestion—he called his new Russian friend and informed him what was happening on the island. He told Dmitri he had instructed his security team to increase their numbers, but beyond that, he didn't know what to do. Dmitri asked him a few questions about what they wanted and all the attempts made to get rid of him. Dmitri asked if Henry would go down there to face the man, but he said he had no plans to do that, concerned that if he showed his face, he may get killed.

"Sometimes these men need a firm refusal from the leader in order to listen, Henry. George...he does not have that strong of presence. But if you go there, look the man in the eye and tell him to take the money and get the hell out, or face the consequences...you might be surprised at the impact."

The consequences. Henry felt heat drifting up his neck. He threatened Jaku when he alluded to harming Lydia, and he meant it then. Now he had to ask himself if he could take up this banner and require his people to use extreme force. And if he did that, what chain of events would that set off? Henry felt a sudden headache coming on. "Okay, Dmitri. I'll take your advice. I'll ask George to contact the man...assuming he knows how...and I'll face him."

"Do not worry; this will all pass. Keep your security close during the meeting and make sure the man knows in certain terms that you will not be helping him."

To Dmitri, it was so simple. But for Henry, this was not anything he ever thought he would have to do. He sighed, remembering Lydia's concern that this very thing would happen. He was so sure his plan of offering them business severance would be enough. Apparently, for this particular client, moving the uranium took precedence over easy money.

After hanging up with Dmitri, he went to the nursery to check on baby Geoffrey, who was fast asleep in his crib. The baby looked so peaceful and he wished he could freeze this moment in time. Henry walked into the bathroom where Lydia was. She had finished her bath and was sitting on the edge of the bathtub with a towel wrapped around her body, applying lotion to her legs. He stood in the doorway with his hands in his pockets as he watched her. He felt guilty that he was planning on withholding this from her...but he rationalized that telling her would only cause her to worry and that wouldn't help anything.

She looked up at him and smiled, pulling the pin that held her hair wrapped up in a bun on top of her head as her dark, silky hair cascaded down her back. "What's on your mind, darling?" Lydia stood and walked toward him, placing her hands on his shoulders. "You look weary."

Henry smiled at her. "Just glad to be home," he replied, kissing her on the lips. "I talked to George earlier. There's a prospective client who needs help with moving a shipment of produce from South America. He's requested a meeting before he commits to anything. So, I'll be going back sometime soon." He hated lying to her, and it surprised him how easy it was.

Lydia touched his face. "I understand. Maybe one day when Geoffrey's a little older we can start going with you."

Henry nodded at her. "That would be nice." And he privately hoped that it could be possible. When all of Philip's old criminal clients stop coming out of the woodwork, it would be safe for Lydia and their child.

Within a few weeks, he was back at the estate in the Cayman Islands. He noticed immediately that the size of the security team more than doubled, which pleased him. He found George in the house. It was very late on a Friday night, and he was sitting in the kitchen having a late dinner when Henry arrived. They were both tired and spoke little beyond the standard greeting and pleasantries. Henry had taken a cab straight to the airport after finishing his day at the National Gallery earlier in the afternoon, so to say he was road-weary would be an understatement. Henry told George he could go home and they would re-group first thing in the morning to prepare for their meeting with the Immovable Mr. Uranium, as Henry now called him, not knowing his name or any other details about him; he had created this exaggerated caricature in his mind of a mustache-stroking villain who threw his weight around bullishly.

Henry slept like a rock that night and woke up with a slight travel hangover. He called Lydia first thing and spoke to her until Geoffrey demanded more attention. After hanging up with her, he showered, dressed, and made his way to the kitchen to prepare his breakfast.

George showed up about thirty minutes later and Henry offered him a cup of coffee, which he accepted. They sat in the kitchen drinking coffee and discussing the advice Dmitri gave him. George agreed that the man might stand down if the appropriate pressure was applied. Henry told him he was nervous and truly hoped that it would work.

"Davis mentioned he might be able to help you set the stage. Maybe you should talk to him?"

"Set the stage?" Henry asked, curious what that meant and how the security team lead could help him do that.

"Talk to him," was George's simple response.

Henry looked at George and nodded. "Alright, I will. As soon as I finish my coffee."

"I'll fetch him for you," George said without hesitation, and before Henry could stop him, he left the kitchen with haste.

Henry was still sipping his coffee minutes later when George returned to the kitchen, with Davis following close behind. Henry surveyed him, as if for the first time. Davis was tall, roughly the same height as he was. He remembered hearing that he was a retired Green Beret in the US Army. Davis was probably in his late thirties, with light brown hair and sun-darkened skin. He wore a short beard on his face and had tattoos on his biceps. He nodded in greeting at Davis. "Good morning, Davis."

"Good morning, Sir. You wanted to see me?" Davis stood at attention.

Henry glanced at George and grinned. "Well... two things: first, thanks for building up the security team; I appreciate your responsiveness."

Davis nodded once. "It's my job, Sir. Happy to help."

Henry smiled. "The second thing...I hear you might have some advice for me regarding our impending visitor."

Davis quickly obliged, sharing his thoughts with Henry about ways to carry himself and improve the perception of those who wished to intimidate him. He also insisted that Henry wear a side-arm, which he strongly opposed at first, having never handled a gun before, but Davis was convincing. He assured Henry he would never have to remove it from the holster and would even remove the bullets if that made him feel better about it. Henry begrudgingly agreed, though he opted to leave it loaded. Davis retrieved a black shoulder holster and a 9MM pistol from his vehicle. He helped Henry with the fitting of the holster, ensuring the straps were secure and it would not move. Davis then inspected the pistol closely, ejecting the magazine to see how many bullets were in it, confirming again with Henry that he wanted to leave it loaded. He slapped the magazine back into the gun and checked to make sure a bullet was not chambered, then pressed the safety button and told Henry to raise his left arm. He slid the gun into the holster. "How does it feel?" Davis asked, giving the straps at the shoulders a final tug to make sure they were secure.

"Strange..." Henry said, resting his arm gingerly in place.

"You'll get used to it," Davis responded with a friendly punch to the shoulder. "Remember what I told you. Me and a few other guys will be with you. He'd be a dumb ass to try anything with us in there."

Henry grinned. "Thank you, Davis." With a nod, Davis left the kitchen to return to his duty post. He took what Davis said to heart and practiced the body language he recommended, seeing an odd element of humor in the whole situation.

CHAPTER 11

HIDDEN TALENTS

Henry's ears were ringing when he opened his eyes. He was confused, sprawled across the floor, which was covered in glass shards from the shattered windows in the office. He turned his head and saw George curled up on his side, his eyes shut tight and his hands pressed firmly over his ears. Henry could hear shouting and gunfire, but in his confusion could not comprehend what was happening. His head hurt. He touched the back of his head and felt the warm, sticky presence of blood. Rising to his feet, shaking and unsteady, he leaned against the desk as his head spun. He staggered to the door, willing his mind to grasp what his ears heard and his eyes saw.

There were a handful of bodies lying on the ground—some men he recognized from his security team, some he didn't recognize. The gunfire had slowed and then stopped; he could hear muffled shouting as he slogged his way to the front door, fighting off dizziness and nausea.

The front door was wide open and he could smell smoke and something else he didn't recognize. He stepped outside and saw several of his security team members shouting back and forth at each other as they tended to two men lying on the ground. Henry looked around again and saw more bodies outside. He could no longer control his nausea and threw up near a large tropical plant along the front of the house. He was doubled over and spitting when he felt a hand on his shoulder. "Are you okay, Sir?"

Henry looked at Davis, noting that he was drenched with sweat and bleeding from a few cuts on his face, but otherwise seemed unharmed. "What the hell happened? I don't remember anything," Henry said, touching the back of his head again.

Davis looked at his head and brought him to sit down inside. "You probably have a concussion, Sir." Henry obeyed, allowing Davis to lead him to the parlor, which was relatively unscathed; no broken windows or dead bodies in there. Davis then described the events of the last thirty minutes.

Apparently, the Immovable Mr. Uranium returned. His name was actually Eduardo Comal Castañeda, a disgraced commander from the Guatemalan military who had turned to a life of insidious full-time crime after his very public ouster from the military. Turns out he was caught selling retired military assets, virtually out the backdoor of an armory, to customers that Philip may well have been acquainted with. Señor

Castañeda arrived with a decent entourage of gun-toting men. They escorted him to the office with two of his men, where he and Henry met. Davis explained that Henry did very well during the meeting and did not back down when Señor Castañeda tried to intimidate him. "You were a natural, Sir," Davis explained. Ultimately, Castañeda left, refusing to be paid off, declaring that he would find someone else to deliver the uranium. "And that's when the shit hit the fan." Davis looked over his shoulder at the bodies in the foyer that were visible from the parlor. As Castañeda and his men were walking to the door, he pulled his gun and pointed it at Henry. "But, Sir, without hesitation, you drew your weapon, racked it, and shot him first...twice in the chest. I nearly shit myself. You said you'd never handled a gun before, right?"

Henry blinked and his mouth gaped, not knowing what to say. "No..." he stammered. "I've never..." He shook his head, which spun afresh at the movement, and he whimpered.

"Well, regardless, it was pretty bad ass. But then all hell broke loose." Davis explained that the two men who escorted Castañeda opened fire and had to be put down. Also, there were men watching through the windows outside and when they saw Castañeda and the other two go down, they opened fire, shattering the windows, sending glass and bullets everywhere. "We all hit the deck pretty quickly when that started. That must have been when you hit your head." Davis continued the saga, up to when Henry came out the front door and found him. Henry asked about his security team. "We had three casualties." Davis said somberly. "But from what I can tell, we got all of Castañeda's men." Davis put a hand on Henry's shoulder. "One of my guys is a field medic. Rico. I served with him. He's very good. He'll come see you when he's finished tending to the wounded outside."

Henry nodded slowly, trying to be careful not to rattle his brain any more than it already was. He leaned back in the chair he was sitting in, feeling the straps of the holster rubbing against his shoulders. He had shot and killed a man. How did he do that? It had to be dumb luck.

The rest of the day was spent cleaning up the house, with George making a few phone calls to people who have helped in the past, most recently when Lydia got help with the South African drug dealers. Within an hour of George's phone calls, two large vans pulled up and four people got to work gathering bodies, followed by the initiation of repairs to the damages sustained to the house during the shoot-out. Henry observed in silent amazement. Within a few hours, the house appeared as if nothing had happened. By the time the dust settled, it was late, and Henry had missed his opportunity to call Lydia.

That night, he did not sleep well, worried about the state of his head injury. As he laid in bed staring at the ceiling, a memory floated to the surface...something long forgotten, but when it came, it answered one question, only to prompt about a thousand more.

In the memory, Henry was a young boy. He was walking through the corridors of the school he attended in Moscow with three other boys who were his friends—Mischa, Yuri, and Mikael. There were no windows in the corridor, and he recognized it was the basement level of the school. The four boys arrived at a solid metal door at the end of the hallway and knocked. A man wearing military garb opened the door; it wasn't a dress uniform, more like fatigues. He greeted them, speaking Russian, and let them into the room. It was a large, cavernous space. The walls were made of bricks or stone, and the floor was concrete. The man talked to them, describing "today's lesson" as he led them all to a steel table, waist-high, that was covered with a variety of firearms. One-by-one, he asked the boys to approach the table, choose a gun, and fire at the mannequin targets that had been set up at the far end of the space. The man actively coached them as they shot their respective dummies. After each boy finished, he escorted them down the range to inspect what they had done. Henry remembered touching the rubbery surface of the dummy he had shot, smiling proudly at his accuracy, and accepting praise from the man who stood beside him.

When all the boys had their turn, they were brought back to the steel table and instructed to disassemble and clean the guns they had used. When they finished, the military man called over a man sitting in the corner that Henry didn't notice before that moment. Henry stood shoulder to shoulder with the other boys and watched this man approach. He had gray hair and mustache, glasses, and wore a simple wool suit. The memory then got very fuzzy, and the last thing Henry remembered was the man counting and snapping his fingers.

Chapter 12

An Education

The next day, Henry called his dad first thing in the morning, asking about the memory. His dad's response confused him further. "No, Henry; you weren't signed up for anything like that in Moscow...or anywhere, for that matter. Are you sure it wasn't something you saw in a movie?"

Henry scratched at his forehead. He was sure it wasn't a dream or from a movie. He was sure it was a memory. Henry didn't want to worry his dad, so he conceded to his suggestion. "You're probably right, Dad." They talked for a few more minutes about the usual: Lydia, Geoffrey, the National Gallery, then they hung up.

Henry called Lydia and apologized profusely for not calling her last night. She wasn't terribly upset but announced that she was ready for him to come home. Geoffrey was getting very close to walking, and she wanted Henry to be there when it happened.

When he wrapped up his call with Lydia, he went to the kitchen for a cup of coffee and drank it with a couple of aspirin to help with the lingering headache. He went outside and found Davis at his usual post. Henry asked him if he could set up a shooting course; he felt strange making the request, but he needed to know if what happened with Castañeda was a fluke or not. Davis agreed and pointed out an abandoned horse barn on the estate grounds, saying that he would have it set up there. "Give me an hour, Sir. I'll get it ready for you."

An hour later, Henry met Davis at the horse barn and found several targets set up. From glass bottles in a variety of sizes, to round metal plates on a target apparatus, to human-sized paper targets set up at various distances. He spotted Davis, who was holding the same shoulder holster Henry wore yesterday.

"Let's put this back on you," Davis said as he approached Henry, taking a step behind him. After sliding the holster up Henry's arms and onto his shoulders, helping him put it in place, Davis pulled a gun from the waistband of his pants and put it in the holster. "Do you want earplugs?"

Henry looked down the range at the targets and then at the pistol at his side. He took stock of the state of his headache and thought it would be wise to mitigate it worsening as much as possible. "Yes, please."

Davis opened a pocket on the tactical vest that he wore and pulled out two small, oblong, spongy earplugs and handed them to Henry. "Here. They're clean; never been used."

Henry nodded and took them, rolling and inserting them into his ears. He stepped up to where Davis indicated as the ideal shooting distance and looked at the targets again.

"Whenever you're ready, Sir," Davis shouted from a slight distance behind Henry.

Henry pulled the pistol from the holster and held it in his hand. He found the safety switch and toggled it off. Holding the gun felt strange; his palms started sweating, and his pulse accelerated. He raised the gun and aimed it at the metal plate targets and fired six times, once for each plate, hitting them all as they collapsed backwards on the target frame. Henry moved on to the bottles, and they shattered one-by-one. He finished with the paper targets alternating between center mass and head shots until he ran out of bullets.

He stood there holding the smoking pistol, taking deep breaths, his eyes wide with realization: he could shoot...and he could shoot very well. Henry put the gun back in the holster and scratched his chin as he walked down the range to inspect the paper targets he shot. He touched the holes in the center mass of one target and blinked. His eyes dropped to the ground and closed, recalling the memory from last night, willing his brain to show him more...wanting to re-experience the memory and more like it.

He felt two hands clap him on his shoulders, then opened his eyes to see Davis standing next to him smiling, speaking, though his words were muffled. Henry pulled the plugs out of his ears and forced a grin. "Well done, Sir; well done!" Davis said enthusiastically.

He nodded. "Thanks, Davis. This was educational."

Chapter 13

Looking for Answers

Twenty-four hours later, Henry was back in London, determined to contact the three boys from his memory. He remembered their names and gave them to George before he left, asking him to help track them down. He wanted to know if they could help him fill in the blanks.

Two weeks later, George contacted Henry with an update. He told him that two of the boys were dead. "One died in a motorcycle accident three years ago in Budapest," George explained.

"Budapest? Three years ago?" Henry scratched his forehead. "Damn. I was in Budapest for work... it was about three years ago, too." He shook his head. "What about the other one?"

"The other was killed in a mugging last year in Prague. What are the odds? Such a shame; two young lives gone." George concluded.

Henry's brow furrowed as he remembered the very short trip he took to Prague for a seminar on Bohemian art last year. The night before he returned to London, he'd had one too many shots of slivovice with his Czech counterparts. He woke up with the worst sort of hangover the next morning.

"The last one alive is Mischa Burov. My source told me he was assigned to the Russian Embassy in London earlier this year, but doing what, he didn't know."

Henry thanked him for the information and couldn't believe his luck that Mischa was in London, too. He wasn't certain what the protocol would be to visit a Russian Embassy, but he resolved to visit, anyway. He needed answers, and he hoped Mischa could provide them.

The next day after work, Henry took a cab from the National Gallery, which dropped him off in front of the Embassy at around 4:30 p.m. He stood at the front gate, looking through the bars at the historical building on the other side. Henry stepped through the gate and was stopped almost instantly by a man in a black suit standing off to the side, who had been concealed by a section of brick wall. He spoke English, asking Henry if he could help him. Henry responded to the man in Russian. *"I'm here to see Mischa Burov. He's an old friend, and I recently learned he was here in London."*

The man hesitated, looking at Henry with appraisal. *"What's your name?"* he asked in Russian.

"Henry Coats. Mischa and I were schoolmates in Moscow when we were boys."

The man's expression was neutral. *"Wait here,"* he said as he walked away. Henry watched as the guard entered the building. Several minutes later, the man returned. "*Mischa does not know you. Leave immediately.*" His eyes focused on Henry's face.

Henry was taken aback, then nodded after a long moment of hesitation. "*Of course; I apologize for the disruption.*" Henry put his hands in his pockets and stepped out of the gate and stood on the sidewalk, looking up and down the street for a cab. He felt awkward, sensing that the man was watching him closely, so he walked farther up the lane to hail a cab away from the Embassy. He had walked about half a kilometer when he stopped, again aiming to hail a cab, when a man approached him abruptly, startling him.

"Henry?" the man said.

Henry studied him; he was about his age with light hair and eyes, tall and fit. "Yes?" Henry said, his eyebrows drawn together.

The man studied his face for a moment. "It is you, then."

"I'm sorry; do I know you?" Henry asked with agitation.

"I should think so; you were just at the embassy looking for me, were you not?"

Henry blinked. "Mischa?"

The man nodded once. "Yes."

"You said you didn't know me," Henry pointed out, feeling half relieved, half perturbed by the mixed messages.

Mischa shrugged. "I didn't want to answer questions about you. Your business tends to not be your own at the Embassy."

"I see." Henry relaxed with the explanation.

A smile transformed Mischa's face. "But it is good to see you, Henry! It has been too long."

Henry grinned. "Yes; it has. You look well, Mischa."

"And so do you." Mischa glanced across the street at a pub. "Let me buy you a drink and we can talk."

Henry agreed, and they crossed the street, stepping into a busy Notting Hill pub. They sat at a table opposite the bar, both ordering a pint, then fell into conversation.

"Did you know that Yuri and Mikael are dead?" Henry asked after they passed the standard pleasantries.

Mischa picked up his glass. "I knew." He sipped his beer. "A tragedy."

Henry tried to read Mischa, but he was uncommonly neutral. He wondered how he truly felt about their deaths. "Listen, Mischa...I wanted to talk to you...to ask you some questions. Something happened to me recently...and I remembered something from our school days in Moscow...something that doesn't really make sense. I'm hoping you can help me solve the mystery."

Mischa slowly set his beer down as his eyes focused on Henry's face. "I will try to help if I can."

Henry relayed the events of the memory to Mischa and also told him about his performance on the gun range.

Mischa listened with interest, drinking his beer, nodding along as Henry spoke. When Henry finished, Mischa pulled a cigarette out of his pocket and put it between his lips. "Do you smoke?" Henry shook his head. "Do you mind if I do?" Mischa asked, opening a zippo lighter.

"No; go ahead," Henry lifted his beer to his lips.

Mischa lit the cigarette, took a slow drag, then scratched his eyebrow. "I do not know what to tell you, Henry. I do not share this memory."

Henry paused for a long moment, maintaining eye contact with Mischa. He finally nodded, feeling disappointed that he wouldn't be getting the answers he was hoping for. "It's alright. I get the feeling it was something I was never supposed to remember." Henry chuckled. "It's like something straight out of the Manchurian Candidate...except I'm not an assassin." Henry laughed again.

Mischa grinned and took another deep draw on his cigarette. "So do you have a family, Henry?"

Henry nodded and smiled. "I do; a beautiful wife and son. I'm a lucky man. And you?"

Mischa crushed the tip of his cigarette on the table and blew smoke into the air above his head. "I have to get back to the embassy. It was good to see you again, Henry."

The abrupt finale of their reunion had henry blinking in surprise. "Sure; maybe we can meet up again some other time...since you are here in London."

"I'm afraid I will not be here much longer. I have business that will soon be complete." Mischa stood up and peered down at Henry.

"Ah...well, thanks for stepping out to talk to me. I wish you the best wherever you are headed next."

Henry held out his hand to shake. Mischa took it and Henry noticed a gold chain around his wrist, unique enough that it caught his attention.

They stepped out of the pub and Mischa walked with haste back toward the embassy. Henry watched him for a moment, then saw a black cab approaching, which he hailed.

CHAPTER 14

UNEXPLAINED

At home, Henry told Lydia about the reunion he'd had with his old classmate and how closed off Mischa felt. He remembered him as a jovial boy, a bit of a class-clown during their school days, so this older version of Mischa surprised him. She offered that maybe he had a stressful job that tempered his formerly pleasant personality. Henry felt he had no choice but to forget the memory and move on with his life, resigned to never knowing what it meant.

A week later, Henry left the National Gallery around 8:30 p.m. He had been working late all week, tasked with coordinating the setup of a new exhibit on loan from The Met in New York. They specifically chose him to lead this effort based on his previous history working for The Met. It was a big opportunity and if it went well, he might get a promotion.

It was dark outside, and he got a cab promptly. The ride to his flat was quick, as most of the traffic had died down. The cab stopped in front of his home and he paid the driver, then stepped out of the car. He noticed the streetlight that normally illuminated the front of his building was out and he wondered when it would be fixed. The cab drove away as he approached the front of the building, but a masked figure stepped into his path, startling him. The attacker brandished a knife and told Henry he would kill him unless he gave him his wallet. Henry complied, immediately pulling his wallet out of his pocket and held it out to the man. "Here, take it; it's yours. Please, just take it and go." Henry's eyes focused on the man's concealed face.

The masked man grabbed the wallet and Henry's gaze dropped to the knife held in the man's right hand, and he thought he saw the briefest glint of gold around his wrist.

"Mischa?" Henry gasped, drawing his eyebrows together.

The man hesitated. "Sorry, Henry. It is not personal," the masked man responded as he lunged at Henry with the knife aimed at his gut.

Henry only had half a second to react, and an odd sensation came over him as he blacked out. For a moment he was certain that he was dead, but he blinked and looked around and saw that he was still on the walkway in front of his flat, but the masked man...Mischa...lay motionless on the ground before him.

"Mischa?" He crouched before him. "Mischa?" he whispered frantically. The knife was still in Mischa's hand; Henry kicked it away. Mischa didn't respond, so Henry pressed his fingers to his neck to feel for a pulse, not finding one. Henry cussed. As fortune would have it, a police car was driving past and Henry ran into the road, flailing his arms wildly. The police car screeched to a stop, and the bobbie jumped out, shouting at Henry that he almost got himself killed. Henry ignored the officer's chastisement and called for help. The policeman approached as Henry explained what happened. However, things got strained when Henry couldn't explain why the masked mugger lay dead and he didn't have a scratch on him.

"It sounds crazy, I know. He lunged at me and I... and I...I just don't know. I can't explain it." Henry tried to reason with the man.

"You a Yank?" the officer demanded. "Are you armed? Do you have a gun?"

"No, Sir." Henry stared at Mischa, unable to visually determine the cause of death. He didn't see any blood.

"I have to call for backup...and you'll need to come answer some questions for my superiors." The bobbie stepped back to his car, turned on the flashers, and picked up the handset for the radio in his car.

Henry ran his hands through his hair in disbelief. "Can I please go talk to my wife first? And let her know what's happened? She'll be worried sick if I don't show my face."

The officer didn't respond directly, but spoke into the radio, calling for an ambulance and backup from other officers in the area to investigate a death. He ended the call-out by saying that he was going to escort a person-of-interest to inform his wife that they needed him at the station to answer questions. He put the radio down and closed the door. Two more police cars showed up just then, with lights flashing. They stepped out of their cars and the five officers huddled together to dole out instructions. The first officer on the scene broke away from the group and gave Henry a stern look. "Let's go. I'll give you three minutes to talk to your wife."

Henry turned on his heel and entered the building. The officer followed closely, and Henry could feel the suspicion pulsating off of him. Moments later, he was at his door. He opened it and saw Lydia staring out the window at the lights below. She turned to face him. "Henry! Darling, something's happened." Her eyes were wide and went wider when she saw the officer behind him.

"I know...I was attacked. I have to go with the officer to answer some questions...to help with their investigation." He walked up to her and put his hands on her shoulders.

"You were attacked? I don't understand. Why haven't they arrested the one who attacked you? He's the one who should answer questions." She pressed her hands against his chest, her eyes fervently searching his.

Henry hesitated. "Because he's dead."

The color drained from Lydia's face. "Dead?" She curled her fingers into his shirt. "This doesn't make any sense." Her eyes were welling up with tears.

"I know...but I need to help the officers." Henry looked over his shoulder at the man behind him...

unsure of what guarantee he could give her right now. "I'll be home as soon as I can." He kissed her lips and held her close. "I love you."

"I love you, too. Please hurry back," she replied as tears streamed down her cheeks.

Henry pulled away from her, then turned to the officer and nodded.

Ninety minutes later, Henry was at Scotland Yard, sitting in an interrogation room with the officer and his captain, retelling the version of events for what felt like the fifteenth time. Henry was growing more and more distraught and frustrated at not being able to explain what happened to Mischa. He had told them he realized he knew the man, and they explored that avenue thoroughly.

"Did you owe him money?"

"Did you sleep with his wife?"

"Did he hold a grudge against you for some reason?"

Eventually, the officer and his captain left the room and Henry sat alone, remembering the fear in Lydia's eyes...wondering why this was happening to him. He laid his head on the table, overcome with exhaustion...wishing he was home in bed with his wife. It had been a very long week with everything going on at work and this was salt in the wound.

He must have dozed off because the sound of the door opening startled him. He squinted as his eyes found the Captain in the bright fluorescent lights of the room. The Captain was in his late fifties, with a head of strawberry blond hair and a mustache to match. He was medium build and height and spoke with a Liverpudlian accent. His name was Carson.

Captain Carson sat in a chair opposite from Henry and studied him. "I just heard from the medical examiner. The man who attacked you died by asphyxiation through a crushed windpipe." He looked at Henry as he pulled a small notebook out of his pocket, which he had been using to write notes. "Have you had any martial arts training? Hand to hand combat, Mr. Coats?"

Henry shook his head. "No...never."

"Are you former military?"

"No, Sir...I studied art at Oxford. I work for the National Gallery, for God's sake." Henry held his head in his hands.

"And you're certain no one else was there?"

Henry shook his head. "I saw no one else."

Captain Carson closed his book and sighed. "I believe you. It's a strange situation, to be sure. But I believe you." The Captain tapped his pen on the table. "I think we'll chalk this up to dumb-luck, self-defense." Captain Carson grinned briefly under his bushy mustache. "You're free to go, but here's my card, in case you think of anything else important." He handed him a small white card with his name and phone number on it.

Henry took the card and read it with relief. "Thank you, Sir. I will. Thank you," he repeated, and they stood up together and shook hands.

Captain Carson opened the door to the interrogation room. "Send my regards to the missus." The Captain reached into his coat pocket and pulled out a plastic bag and handed it to Henry. It was his wallet. "This has already been processed and documented, so we don't need it anymore, but you might."

Henry had completely forgotten about his wallet being taken. He took the bag and thanked him again, then left the building and caught a cab quickly, feeling exhausted and relieved to be going home.

Once again in front of his flat for the second time that night, he paid the driver and stepped out of the cab. The streetlight that was out mere hours ago was once again working. Clearly, the police requested that the light be fixed as it likely helped with their investigation.

When he walked through the door to his flat, Lydia greeted him almost immediately. She clung to him, relieved that he was home, asking questions about what happened. He explained as best he could, once more wishing that he could fill in the blanks. The version he shared seemed to be good enough for her. She had spent too much time lingering on the fact that he had been attacked, so she was relieved that he was alive and well, tormented by the possibility of the alternative. She asked him to come to bed, where she initiated an emotionally driven night of lovemaking. The intimacy they shared was a balm that helped to offset how utterly wrong the day went; for the moment, he could forget about what happened and immerse himself in the healing power of Lydia's touch.

CHAPTER 15

A REVELATION

A couple of days later, on Saturday, the post was delivered and there was a letter hand-addressed to Henry. Lydia was in the lounge, playing a tape of nursery rhymes for Geoffrey, who seemed to enjoy them immensely, based on the squeals and baby babble coming from the room. Henry sat at the breakfast table with his coffee and opened the letter.

"Henry,

You are receiving this letter because you bested me. Even as I write this, I do not believe it is possible, and yet it would be unwise to be so arrogant as to disregard even the smallest chance."

Henry stopped reading and his eyes fell to the bottom of the page. *It's from Mischa!*

"When you arrived at the Embassy, I wondered if you had at last come for me, too. But after talking to you, I wondered if you really did not know what you were, or if it was an act.

I told the truth when I told you I did not share the memory you described, but I can tell you what it meant. Since I am dead, there will be no consequences for me.

When we were boys, we were recruited into a new training program developed by the military under the instruction of a renowned psychotherapist from Moscow. The purpose of the program was to fill the pipeline with obedient and skilled defenders of Mother Russia. We were the first and they found a special sort of poetry with you being American born.

I believe the memory you described was a recollection of one of our many daily training sessions. I learned about these training sessions later as an adult, after the KGB recruited me. And I learned that hypnosis-induced amnesia was a critical element of our training. They had screened us before-hand to ensure that our minds were bendable...able to be hypnotized. A bendable mind is a controllable mind, you see.

From what I learned later, you left the program before they could "deactivate" you. So, all the training you took part in up to that point is embedded into your brain, an integral part of your subconscious now.

For those of us that finished the training, we have specific triggers that activate us. But, since you did not finish the training, your triggers are unknown.

The directors of the program were content to forget about you, but when Yuri died, followed by Mikael, they got nervous. The manner in which they died was textbook 'make it look like an accident' assassination. They concluded that one of their own had done this. They took steps to thoroughly investigate myself and others, finding that none of us could have been responsible. And then, they brought up your name. They burned through many resources to track you down and document your patterns, and they learned you were in the same cities as Yuri and Mikael when they died.

You killed Yuri and Mikael. And you likely have no memory of it. The theory is that perhaps you bumped into them casually and then something, God knows what, activated you, hijacking your mind and your body.

It's very interesting that you guessed, albeit jokingly, that you felt like something out of the movies. Truth can be stranger than fiction, no?

When they determined you were responsible for the deaths of Yuri and Mikael, they sent me to London to watch you...to see if I could learn what your trigger might be. Imagine my surprise the day you show up at the embassy, asking for me. I applaud whatever method you used to learn my location. My placement in London is considered "unofficial", therefore the success or failure of my mission was reliant on me and me alone. If I were apprehended for any reason while on this assignment, I would be disavowed...unclaimed...a raving madman who had no connection whatsoever to the Russian government. And now my body will go unclaimed...my mother will never know what happened to her son. This is the life I chose.

I informed my commander that you approached me, and I was instructed to terminate you. You are a liability to the program...a wild card that they decided they could no longer afford to keep in play. And here we are now.

I hope this gives you the answers you seek. I know if I were in your shoes, I would want to know this.

Be careful, Henry. I certainly hope that your programming would never cause you to bring harm to your family.

Yours in death,
Mischa"

CHAPTER 16

EVERYBODY HURTS

Henry's eyes burned, frozen open, unblinking. He didn't know how to process this, and he felt like he was standing on a frozen lake, with the ice cracking violently under his feet. The words in the last paragraph of the letter echoed in his fragile mind. He would never hurt Lydia or Geoffrey...would he? He thought he would be sick.

So much of what Mischa's letter detailed both made sense and made no sense at all.

He killed Yuri and Mikael? Impossible. How could he have no memory of something like that? How could he have no memory of crushing Mischa's windpipe?

If what Mischa wrote was true, there was a dormant part of his brain that could awaken at any time, but what exactly would awaken it? And how could he stop it from ever waking up again? He needed to figure this out, but he could never share this with Lydia, because that would mean telling her that he was a killer. He couldn't do that to her.

Could he seek professional help with this? The thought had no sooner entered his head when he dismissed that as a solution, imagining the introduction: *"Hello, I'm Henry. The Russians programmed me to be an obedient pawn, except that I'm not obedient and am killing at random. Please help me."* They would lock him up for sure.

He folded the letter, put it in his pocket, then stepped into the sitting room and watched Lydia and Geoffrey for several moments, feeling as if his whole world was crashing down around him. He could never hurt them...would never hurt them. Would he? Could he?

Lydia looked up at him and smiled, and he felt the glassy ice surface shatter beneath him at last.

"Darling? Are you alright?" Lydia asked, but he didn't know how to respond. "Henry?"

"I...need to go for a walk. I'm sorry." He responded at last, his voice cracking like the ice that was now yielding to his weight, drowning him in the freezing water below it. Before she could say anything, he opened the door and left, running down the stairwell with haste.

The next few weeks were a strained blur. Once a friendly, charming man, Henry became closed... distant. The knowledge of what he was wrapped him in a cocoon of misery. He felt anger and disdain toward Mischa...he wished he had never known.

This change in him affected Lydia the most. She tried to get him to open up to her...to trust her. She loved him and wanted to help him. But he would not be moved. This was a burden that he must bear alone, and he did not try to reassure her. She often cried herself to sleep, wishing he would talk to her...wishing he would come back to her.

His thoughts were consumed with removing this ticking time bomb from his head, but that meant resources were needed...resources that his position at the National Gallery couldn't afford.

The day he decided to leave his position at the National Gallery and manage Philip's business full-time was a day where he felt focused clarity for the first time in weeks. But it was also a day of tragedy.

Lydia approached him and told him she'd just got home from visiting her midwife. She'd not been feeling herself lately and made an appointment for a check-up. She learned she was eight weeks pregnant...but her midwife could not find a heartbeat. The baby had died, and she would miscarry soon.

Henry didn't know what to say or how to feel and he didn't know how to console her; he was far too focused on himself.

Lydia's eyes flooded with tears and she became angry. "Did you hear what I said, Henry?" He nodded wordlessly and could barely look at her. "And you have nothing to say to me?" The tears fell down her cheeks and her breathing became labored as she sobbed violently.

He sensed he needed to do something, so he reached out and touched her cheek, but it was a touch that lacked warmth or feeling, and when her eyes searched his, she found no trace of the man she loved.

She slapped his hand away and told him to get out. She told him not to come back until he was ready to be her husband again.

He packed a suitcase and said nothing to her...he didn't even acknowledge Geoffrey when he left. Later that evening, he was on a plane to the Cayman Islands, intent on gathering the resources he needed to fix his head.

When he arrived, he instructed George to open a new account in his name only, which would be the primary account for the business going forward. He also instructed George to no longer turn away any of Philip's old clientele.

CHAPTER 17

THE DESCENT

June 15, 1996

Henry stood in the den of his Grand Cayman villa watching the BBC news broadcast with a gnawing in his gut. At 11:17 a.m., a truck bomb was detonated on Corporate Street in Manchester, England.

His eyes were glued to the television screen, in disbelief, watching footage of the billowing smoke, the rubble, emergency responders, and frightened civilians who had been evacuated after the bomb threat was called in. It had only been a few hours since the bomb went off, so details were scarce, but he knew who was responsible.

Six Months Prior

Henry stepped off the gangway from his freighter ship onto the solid dock of the port of Dublin. He checked his watch; he would be meeting with his client in twenty minutes. This was the largest and most ethically challenging transaction he'd engaged in since taking over Phillip's business full time.

The paperwork for the port authority had been prepared as suggested by his client, and everything was proceeding smoothly. He had already instructed the crew to prepare the shipping container for removal from the ship. He walked further up the dock, staring out at the water as he waited.

"Henry!"

He turned and saw Eddie Coogan, who was followed by four others who were typically seen in his wake. Henry was not expecting Eddie but was not surprised he'd been sent to close this transaction.

"Hello, Eddie. It's been a while," Henry said as he held out his hand for a shake.

"The Boss couldn't get away, so here I am," Eddie replied as he took Henry's hand. He then pulled a hand-rolled cigarette out of his pocket and put it between his lips, lighting it. After taking a deep drag, he blew the smoke into the air quickly. "I hear you've got some goodies for us," Eddie continued in his Irish brogue.

Nodding once, Henry glanced at the shipping container that was being taken off the ship at that moment. "I do, indeed. About four-thousand pounds of semtex," Henry said evenly.

Eddie turned to the men behind him with a bright smile, saying something in Gaelic that prompted a laugh from them all.

Henry watched this exchange, remembering the last bombing the IRA carried out in England, but they had declared a ceasefire about a year-and-a-half ago. "So, what are the plans for all this?" Henry asked casually, not expecting a response but felt compelled to ask.

"Oh, just a little fun. Nothing to be concerned about at all," Eddie replied with too bright of a smile.

Henry thought again about the ceasefire. "My wife and son live in England...and I followed your previous bombing campaigns closely."

Eddie laughed. "We've not blown up anything in England in over a year." He caught the eye of one man behind him, who chuckled. "Let's take a look inside, shall we?"

The container was maneuvered onto the empty trailer of a large truck by a crane. Henry approached the trailer and removed the heavy-duty padlock securing the doors of the large metal box. With a loud squeal, he opened the doors and stood back. Eddie climbed into the container and Henry watched as he inspected the contents. After a few moments, Eddie exclaimed something else in Gaelic and came back to the edge, jumping down with a grin.

"You're a gentleman and a scholar, Henry." Eddie held his hand out for another shake. "Allow me to congratulate you on the large deposit that will be sent to your account soon."

Henry wondered how many people were going to get hurt by whatever that semtex would be used for. But he forced a smile as he shook Eddie's hand and suppressed the uneasy feeling churning in his gut, remembering what he needed the money for. He'd connected with a doctor in Brazil who agreed to evaluate him, but it was going to cost him a small fortune. "It's a pleasure doing business with you, Eddie. Send my regards to your boss."

Less than a month after that transaction went down, the ceasefire ended with the bombing of the London Docklands. Two people were killed and over a hundred people were injured.

His eyes burned from staring wide eyed at the television. The Manchester bombing was a day before the match between Russia and Germany in the Euro '96 football tournament; something he'd purchased tickets for Lydia and Geoffrey to attend, knowing that his son loved football. He'd mailed them the tickets a month ago.

I have to call Lydia. I have to make sure she and Geoffrey are okay.

He picked up the phone and dialed her number. It rang and rang until her answering machine picked up, but he didn't leave a message. Not giving up, he called again.

"Hullo?"

"Lydia! I've seen what happened on the news. Are you and Geoffrey all right?"

"Henry?" Shock was audible in her voice. "You've got some bollocks on you," she said in a shout-whisper. "How *dare* you call me and pretend to be concerned? How *dare* you!"

"I was worried about you and Geoffrey; I just wanted—"

"I don't want you to call us anymore. Do you understand? I'll be changing my number, Henry." Her voice trembled, and he could tell she was about to cry. "I mean it, Henry. I never want to hear your voice again. Oh, and I tossed those bloody football tickets into the rubbish bin." She hung up.

Henry stared at the phone as a lump formed in his throat, remembering that the meeting with the Brazilian doctor was a bust. *Was it worth it? Leaving the love of your life and your son behind?*

Was it worth it?

Weeks passed, then months, which eventually turned to years. Henry entertained business offers of all kinds...good, bad, and ugly. He had changed so much that his security team even realized an overhaul. Davis and his men were eventually replaced with others whose ethical code was a bit more pliable, either voluntarily or by force.

He ignored repeated petitions of divorce from Lydia, but he learned she had successfully changed their son's name. He was no longer Geoffrey Coats; he was now Pravin Nagra, son of Priya Nagra.

Ironically enough, his business dealings became increasingly more ruthless and his apparent preference for chaos, death, and destruction eventually earned him the nickname "The Crocodile".

In time, Henry regained the charming, friendly parts of himself, reserving them only for when it suited him. He told no one what he was set to accomplish and pursued wealth at all costs in order to find the solution he desperately wanted...control over his own mind once again.

Now and then, he would return to England to see his son. Often it was while he was at school, since Henry was unable or unwilling to face Lydia. But by then, The Crocodile had earned so much notoriety that he had to be careful.

He kept apprised of developments in the psychotherapy community, keeping his ear to the ground and pursuing anything that he thought would help him. Periodically, he would be overcome with the crushing weight of regret and remorse for what he did to Lydia and Geoffrey... for abandoning them, for not leaning on her. When this would happen, he would simply polish off an entire bottle of Dmitri's vodka and find an adversary to shoot to distract himself from the pain that festered inside him.

He would also do greedy, reckless things, like kidnapping the daughter of an Israeli government official and her friends, or follow a young woman in Washington DC in order to glean if she'd made him or not. These were just examples of times when his pain dwelt close to the surface...pain that would suffocate him if he didn't do something drastic to put it out of his mind.

Epilogue

H enry studied his son's face, recognizing shock and sadness in his eyes. He occupied his hands by holding the glass tumbler tightly, before setting it on a nearby accent table.

"Dad...?" Pravin said quietly. "Why..." he paused, "why now? Why didn't you tell me sooner?"

He sighed. "That's a hard question to answer. The best I can offer is that the time just never seemed right. I honestly never thought I would tell you, but then you ran into your drug problems some years back...and that was the first time I considered it. I wanted you to know I could relate...when your mind or body doesn't feel like your own..."

Pravin ran a hand across his face roughly and dropped his eyes. "I never would have recovered without the rehab facility you placed me in," he murmured. "I never would have been able to have the career I wanted without getting clean first."

Henry nodded. "And I am so proud of you...and what you've accomplished. Getting clean and staying clean all this time."

"Have you…" Pravin started, then hesitated. "Have you been able to find someone who can help you? Can help, I don't know, wipe out what the Russians put in your head?"

"I learned about a Chinese doctor that is working on a special type of therapy…it sounds like it might be something that would help. He'll be leading a public lecture in a few months that I'm hoping to attend. To hear in person what exactly he's doing and how the trials are going." Henry held eye contact with his son. He had high hopes for the Chinese doctor's experimental treatment. He just wanted to see it work on others before he could volunteer himself.

"Does that mean…" Pravin paused and took a breath. "If you get the help you need…if you are, I dunno, cured…does that mean you'll stop? Doing what you do, I mean."

Henry's heart wrenched as he flashed back to the day he and Lydia sat in the pub and she described how she'd begged her father to abandon his business…remembering the exposure she and her mother had endured. He didn't know how to answer Pravin, so he responded the best way he could. "Possibly; we'll have to see."

"What can I do to help, Dad?" Pravin asked and his eyes were glassy.

"You can't, son." Henry forced a smile. "Try not to worry; I'll get this monkey off my back one way or another."

Pravin exhaled audibly, his expression troubled. "Please let me know if there's ever anything—" He broke off in order to halt the sob that was about to escape his throat. "If there's ever anything I can do. I love you, Dad."

Henry swallowed hard. "I love you, too, Pravin."

Coming Soon

Stay tuned for book 4 of *The Evangeline Series* which will be released Spring 2022.

Follow me on Instagram (@AstridAurelius) or sign up for my newsletter at www.IndieAuthorAstrid.com for updates!

Thank You for Reading

I sincerely hope you enjoyed *Henry*. Please consider leaving a review on Goodreads and Amazon (or whichever site you bought it from). Reviews help independent authors, like me, get the word out about our books. So, please know how much I appreciate your review!

Also, the biggest compliment you can give an author is to tell your friends and family to read their book. If you enjoyed this book, please also consider recommending it to others.

For information about future releases, please subscribe to my newsletter at www.IndieAuthorAstrid.com.

Acknowledgments

Thank you to my family and friends. I couldn't have gotten this far without your encouragement.

To my beta readers: Malin, Alex, Victoria, and Tiffany. Once again, your feedback helped me focus my efforts on the right kind of revisions to make. Thank you!

To Tiffany Andrea, my line editor: I really appreciated your expertise and help with cleaning this up. Thanks again; you're a rock star!

To Lena Yang: thank you for another great cover design.

AMDG.

About the Author

I have been writing casually for years and first discovered a love of writing my senior year in high school. When I went to college, I continued writing in English classes required by my degree plan, which I enjoyed, but opted to major in Accounting because, you know, Accountants have stable careers.

I eventually became a CPA...and taught myself how to drink whiskey—those two things *might* be related.

My writing style is pretty conversational; I don't take myself too seriously. I enjoy writing about things I know like hiking, drinking wine, and being socially awkward.

I prefer to write long-hand and type it up later and have been known to write in the bathtub with a full glass of wine handy.

I live in Round Rock, Texas with my husband, three kids, and two geriatric pups.

You can connect with me on:

https://www.indieauthorastrid.com

https://www.instagram.com/astridaurelius

Also by Astrid Aurelius

The Evangeline Series: Persist

Persist has been recognized as a **B.R.A.G. Medallion Honoree** by IndieBRAG and was a Finalist in the Independent Author Network Book of the Year awards.

Four hikers are missing and Sam is determined to find out what happened to them. However, Ben Baxter, her new boss, stands between her and forward progress.

Sam—focused, headstrong, and a recovering social recluse—needs to earn the respect of her new boss, Benjamin Baxter. But her stubborn need to always be in control and self-reliant plagues her.

Ben—smart, handsome, but painfully aloof—has to navigate his new role as a leader while satisfying his need to be in the field. Will Ben give Sam a chance to prove herself?

Sam and Ben—two people from two different worlds—collide unexpectedly under a shared purpose at Hampton National Forest. What will they learn? How will they grow and change? And to what lengths are they willing to go to get what they want?

THE EVANGELINE SERIES: COLLIDE

Sam's story continues...

She had him.

Charles: the man responsible for the missing hikers.

He even confirmed that he'd killed them. She had Charles. And Ben let him go.

Her mission was clear: Find the John Doe responsible for the missing hikers and make an arrest. She had pictured coming back into the office in triumph, excited to prepare her report and close this case. She imagined testifying at the trial and hearing the gavel come down on his life sentence as the hikers' family members cried and hugged each other in relief, having answers and justice at last. But that would never happen. And Ben was responsible...

But she soon learns that what Ben did was more complex than the simple betrayal she'd labeled it.

THE EVANGELINE SERIES: CATALYST

How do you proceed when you are betrayed by someone you trusted? Ask Sam.

When she discovers someone she had considered a friend is the son of The Crocodile-- the criminal mastermind she's tasked with capturing--she has to proceed with caution, not raising suspicion that she knows who he is or what he's done.

Evangeline Sampierre may be fierce, intense, independent, and strong, but trying to keep herself from The Crocodile's jaws is going to take everything she has.

As she and Ben not only proceed to dismantle the empire of a dangerous criminal, they also have to fight for their relationship. Disagreements, differences, and danger push them to their limits, both personally and professionally. Can their partnership withstand the weight of the world on their shoulders? Can their love strengthen them through the sacrifices they each have to make?

Can they stop The Crocodile?

www.ingramcontent.com/pod-product-compliance
Lightning Source LLC
Chambersburg PA
CBHW020045310726
48970CB00007B/2420